"I CAN'T HEAR YOU !"

A Marines Journey Through Parris Island And The Korean War

By *[signature: Jack Orth] 2015*

JACK ORTH

authorHOUSE

1663 LIBERTY DRIVE, SUITE 200
BLOOMINGTON, INDIANA 47403
(800) 839-8640
www.authorhouse.com

First published by AuthorHouse 06/16/04

ISBN: 1-4184-0788-7 (e)
ISBN: 1-4184-0787-9 (sc)

Library of Congress Control Number: 2004093229

Printed in the United States of America
Bloomington, Indiana

This book is printed on acid-free paper.

PREFACE

In June of 1950, most Americans knew next to nothing about Korea. For the next three years over 34,000 American and U.N. troops were killed, over 100,000 wounded, and 8,000 are still unaccounted for. When a cease fire was declared on July 27th of 1953, the so-called 'Forgotten War' became a war that never really happened in the minds of the majority of Americans.

As time goes by, and the 54th anniversary of the beginning of the war is this year, those who served and survived will never forget time spent in the bitter cold and savage heat of Korea. To them, the war will never be a forgotten one, and their comrades will always be in their thoughts.

Although Jack Harrington and others in the book are fictitious characters, the experiences they encounter are true to life. This book is dedicated to the real life Marines they represent.

ACKNOWLEDGEMENTS

Without the ongoing help and support of my wife, Sally, publishing this book would not have been possible. My love and gratitude go out to her.

Chapter 1

It was like the grand finale of the Fourth of July fireworks display, but the screaming and yelling wasn't to celebrate Independence Day. Never ending explosions threw dirt, rocks, shrapnel, and bodies everywhere. The smell of cordite and the local meat market was in the one-hundred-degree air. The stench burned into the throat and inner soul of Jack Harrington as his six foot frame bent with the weight of Donny "Bee Bop" Harris over his shoulder.

A navy corpsman lowered Harris to the ground, and Jack wished he could share the morphine he pumped into Harris's torn up body.

A few days before, Bee Bop, who billed himself as the colored man's answer to John Wayne in *The Sands of Iwo Jima*, had put it right.

"Those fucking Chinese are like the old bull and the young bull looking down the hill at all the cows. The young bull says, 'Let's run down and fuck one of those cows.' The old bull says, 'Let's walk down and fuck 'em all!'"

The Chinese weren't in any great hurry. They were going to slowly pound the First Marine Division with thousands of rounds of incoming with one goal in mind. That was to drive them off the main lines back into South Korea and into the ocean.

In the middle of all the panic, fear, confusion, and heroism stood Gunnery Sergeant William Parker, as if he were playing war games back at Camp Lejeune, North Carolina. If you looked up United States Marine in the dictionary, you'd see a picture of Gunny Parker! He calmly directed Korean Service Corps people with stretchers to move up the slope to the trench lines to help with the wounded marines.

"Harrington, take some of these gooks up to the Second Platoon area. The shit's hit the fan!"

"O.K., Gunny. Let's move out!" screamed Jack.

The group of Koreans was huddled together in fear, and wanted no part of heading up the hill. Gunny Parker did the perfect imitation of Wyatt Earp at the O.K. Corral.

Standing at the ready position like a western gunfighter, and in drill instructor fashion, he announced, "If you people want to live to see us save your sorry-ass country, move up that fucking slope on the double!"

The Gunny always did have a way with words, and the KSC people took off at triple time.

Like the too-close lightening from a summer storm crashing around your house, the incoming exploded with deafening death. Two Koreans in front of Jack were blown into the air and floated like scarecrows before landing like a sack of ripped open potatoes. The air was sucked out of Jack's lungs, and his head felt like Bob Feller had hit him with a fastball. He was in the meat market again, and thought that smell like freshly cut beef would be his last!

In a daze, with his left leg and shoulder beating like a drum, he checked the six Koreans. None would ever work the rice paddies of South Korea again. Stumbling down the slope through the dust, smoke and crashing incoming toward the command post, he heard the Gunny's voice.

"Fast fucking trip, Harrington!" as he dragged Jack into the C.P. bunker.

The flak jacket was splattered with shrapnel, and surely saved his life.

With a half-smile breaking his usual stone face, the Gunny announced, "They're million dollar wounds, Harrington. You'll be off line and between clean sheets while we're kicking some ass up here in Gooneyland."

Two Charlie Company tanks rolled into the area of the C.P. Gunny Parker yelled up to the tank commander that he had a passenger for him to take down the road to the aid station. He pushed Jack up onto the tank toward the hatch. With incoming everywhere, the Gunny acted like he was at the 7-11 store for a pack of smokes.

"Harrington, throw down your cigarettes! You'll have plenty where you're going!"

With the Camels in midair, the only sounds were explosions, but the eye-to-eye contact said it all as the tank cranked up and moved out.

"Who the hell was that masked man? It must be the Lone Ranger!" yelled the tank commander.

Jack knew that the Lone Ranger and Tonto together were no match for the Gunny.

The aid station was a zoo. Wounded Marines were everywhere, and in a nearby area dead Marines were stacked like cordwood. Among the wounded Marines were two badly hit Chinese prisoners. One Marine volunteered his medical services.

"Doc, just give me a weapon. I'll kill those two fuckers and save ya some time!"

A navy doctor checked Jack over, and the corpsman, with his own touch of genius, added to Jack's painless lightheadedness with a jolt of painkiller.

The helicopter looked like a plastic bubble with a huge propeller on top. On each side was a basket-like stretcher. As Jack was strapped in for the flight to the hospital ship *U.S.S. Repose* anchored off the Korean coast, the magic of morphine and the stuttering sound of the chopper lulled Jack Harrington into dreams of a different time and place.

The William Tell Overture floated out of the small Arvin radio in his bedroom as a deep voice crooned, "From out of the past come the thundering hoofbeats of the great horse, Silver. The Lone Ranger rides again!"

Chapter 2

For a seventeen-year-old kid, who had little or no desire to crack the books, the first glimmer of spring was like an engraved invitation to take some time off from the daily grind of the senior year of high school. Jack Harrington gazed out the window as the guidance counselor told him once again he was on thin ice, and might not graduate with the Class of 1950 at Newton High School.

Every kid in school always dreaded any session with Mr. Morgenstern, whose short, plump body was topped off by a bowling-ball smooth head. His froglike eyes were magnified three times over through coke-bottle thick glasses. Thin lips hardly opened when he spoke, and everyone knew he'd hiss his two favorite questions during your session.

"Do you smoke?"

"Do you masturbate?"

Most kids stammered, turned red, and said, "No, Sir" to both questions, so it was great news when word spread about what Billy Fitz and Frankie Lane told him. When Mr. Morgenstern said, "Billy, do you masturbate?" Billy very calmly looked him in the eye. "Oh, no, Mr. Morgenstern. I understand it makes you short and bald!"

When Frankie was asked, he said, "Oh, no, Mr. Morgenstern. I understand it makes hair grow on the palm of your hand!" Frankie swore that Morgenstern glanced at his own upturned palm to check for hairs!

"Mr. Harrington, are you listening to me? I'm recommending that you stay after school each day for the voluntary study program. You don't seem to accomplish anything at home, so supervised study should be of help to you. By the way, do you smoke?"

"No, Mr. Morgenstern."

"Do you masturbate?"

The joke about the kid who was caught jerking off by his mother flashed through Jack's mind.

"Johnny, don't ever do that again. It will cause blindness," said the mother.

"But, Mom, can't I just do it until I need glasses?" pleaded Johnny.

8

"Oh, no, Mr. Morgenstern. I understand it can affect your eyesight in later years!"

Thinking of his quick response to Morgenstern, Jack smiled as he looked into the mirror before going downstairs for dinner. Thoughts of his grandfather widened the grin as the wonderful Irish brogue floated through his mind.

"Jackie Boy, you were blessed with your mother's good looks, and your Uncle Sean's gift of the blarney. Your hair is as black as Hitler's heart, and your smile flashes like the light at the end of the tunnel. They'll stand you in good stead, but life is no bowl of cherries for any of us. With a little Irish luck, hard work, and keeping away from the devil's brew, you can write your own ticket to success.

"The downfall of many an Irishman has been sipping too many Jamieson's followed by pints of Guinness. Don't be like me wonderful brother, Jim, who only drank when he was alone or with somebody. Perhaps, a taste on special occasions may be in order, but be content to watch the others make fools of themselves."

The smell of pot roast replaced thoughts of his grandfather, as the family sat down for dinner. Jack's father asked how school went that day. The Depression of the late 1920's and early 1930's had beaten Mr. Harrington down, and his own struggles to put himself through college seemed wasted on him. None the less, he pushed, along with Jack's mother, for him to attend college.

"Jack, I have an appointment with Mr. Kaplan again to talk about your problems with math. College is probably out of the question next year, but with a year in prep school after graduation, you'll be able to enter college the following year. If only you'd put half the effort into math that you do memorizing baseball averages, it wouldn't be necessary for me to see Mr. Kaplan," smiled Mrs. Harrington.

His father marveled at Jack's uncanny ability to retain anything about baseball. He could tell you the batting average of every Red Sox player on a daily basis, and all the rest of the American and National league players. He knew more about Ted Williams than 'Teddy Ballgame' knew about himself, but ask him what the square root of any number was or how to spell Mississippi, and you'd draw a blank look. Of course, he would tell you that the Mississippi ran through St. Louis, where Stan 'The Man' Musial played for the Cardinals, and Mort and Walker Cooper were the only brother battery in baseball.

"Somehow Jack will work things out in this world of ours," mused his father.

Chapter 3

Mr. Kaplan is the exact opposite of mealy-mouthed Morgenstern, thought Jack.

He was a tall, good-looking man, and treated every student with a smile and a helping hand. After Jack failed the last math test, Mr. Kaplan's comments to Jack were from the heart, and meant to help him.

"Jack, even Ted Williams strikes out now and then, and he doesn't get a hit every time he comes to bat. However, he continues to study hitting, and constantly takes batting practice. Take a page from Ted's book and keep working at it!"

"Please sit down, Mrs. Harrington. It's a pleasure to see you again."

"Mr. Kaplan, I know Jack is in great danger of not graduating with his class, and I'm wearing my heart on my sleeve as I ask a great favor of you. You and I know he's not college material at this point, and may never be. However, I've met with the Dean of Admissions at Huntington Prep School in Boston, and we've enrolled him for next year. Perhaps he'll buckle down and be able to enter college the year after. If his friends graduate without him, I think it will change his life, and lead to all kinds of problems for him."

With a look of admiration, and sincerity in his voice, the words flowed from Mr. Kaplan.

"You know, Mrs. Harrington, Jack is very fortunate to have a mother who loves, understands, and looks out for him. My job as a teacher is to do the best I can to get students ready for the long road ahead of them, and the many hills and curves they'll face. I agree with you that for Jack not to graduate this year will make that road more difficult. You can count on his passing my math class."

As they shook hands, Mr. Kaplan smilingly said, "Besides, is it really important that he knows six plus five is twelve?"

Jack never knew that his mother was really the deciding factor, as he marched up to get his diploma on a warm June evening. The engraved Waltham watch his parents presented to him said it all on the back … "Love and congratulations – June 1950". As far as Jack was concerned, the new watch ticked away toward a new and exciting time as he headed for Cape Cod.

Chapter 3

Carol Anderson had invited Jack to a weekend graduation party at her parent's summer house. Jim Emery, his girlfriend, Judy, and Carol and Jack headed to the Cape in Jim's customized 1941 Ford convertible with double pipes.

Billy Fitz put it best when he heard Jack was the lucky guy going with Carol.

"You lucky bastard! I'd give my left nut to be in your shoes. Charlie Coffey swears she gave him a hand job after the senior prom. Tell her what you told Morgenstern, and she might even let you dip your wick for a graduation present!"

About forty kids spent the weekend at the Anderson's. Her parents cooked breakfast, and tried to keep an eye on the new graduates. They were nowhere in sight when Carol and Jack walked the beach and shared a beer in the sand dunes. One thing lead to another, and if Jack had thought to check his new watch it would have ticked off about fifteen seconds for the actual presentation of the graduation gift to take place, and end.

Carol whispered, "Tell Morgenstern that you've graduated from hand jobs to the real thing, and your eyesight is perfect!"

They worked on increasing the fifteen-second time at bat on many occasions during the summer, and actually worked up to practically a full inning.

Chapter 4

The front-page story in the June 26th, 1950 issue of *The Boston Herald* told about seven North Korean divisions, supported by tanks and aircraft, invading the southern Republic of Korea.

"Sunday, June 25th, the North Korean forces achieved complete surprise as they crossed the 38th parallel into South Korea. Through the monsoon rains came a well-trained North Korean Peoples army of 130,000 strong. Ten infantry divisions armed with the latest Soviet equipment, including T-34 tanks, are heading for the South Korean capitol of Seoul. With little resistance, they're expected to hit Seoul within a week."

That same Monday, Jack and Jim Emery headed for Augusta, Maine with a truckload of insulation for the crew to install in new buildings on a military base there. Jack's father owned a small insulation company, and Jack delivered stock to many jobs for him. Delivering insulation and learning to install it was great fun as far as Jack was concerned, and he couldn't wait to get on the road each time his father needed him.

The first stop was at an insulation factory in Hyde Park. Mr. Buckley, the manager of the plant, was a miserable bastard, and always greeted them in the same fashion.

"Where's Harold, and why aren't you fucking kids in school?"

"Tell him to stick it up his ass," Jim whispered to Jack.

Jack smiled and said, "My father isn't feeling well today, Mr. Buckley, and since Jim and I graduated a few days ago, we're helping him out. We'll be working all summer, and hope to save enough money to help out with college costs in the fall. I'll tell Dad you said 'hello'."

As they loaded the truck, Jim said, "You know if bullshit was music, you'd be able to write a fucking symphony!"

They finished loading, leaving with a "Thanks, Mr. Buckley. It's always nice to see you." They laughed as they headed toward Maine.

"I can't wait to see Bob Langer again," said Jim.

Bob Langer was the foreman of the insulation crew, and one tough guy ... but, liked to see Jack and Jimmy. Bob had served in the Marine Corps on Iwo Jima and other islands in the Pacific during World War II. He looked like the actor John Garfield ... dark, handsome, and always ready for action.

16

Bob and his crew were insulating some new barracks being built at a military facility in Augusta. The barracks were huge, and the deadline for completion was in a week or two. As the electricians did the wiring, the insulators were right behind them, and behind them were the rock lathers. The lathers nailed the plasterboard on the walls and ceilings with black, shiny nails that were treated with some kind of coating.

The nails came in wooden kegs, and the lathers would fill their aprons with nails, … then fill their mouth with the nails. They could spit nails out one by one into their left hand, then hit them with one shot and they'd be through the plasterboard. By the end of every day, each lather would have a black coating all around his lips. The crew of lathers, but especially one guy, was constantly yelling at the insulators to work faster … which, of course, they couldn't do because they had to wait for the electricians to do their work.

Bob Langer had a Marine Corps emblem tattoo on his right forearm, which looked like he was born with it in place.

The lather kept saying, "Hurry up, jarhead. You're holding us up!"

After hearing that for a few days, Bob walked over to the guy, with his staple gun in his hand, and said, "One more fucking word from you, and I'll staple your pecker to the wall! Do you understand me, fuckface?"

Then, one of the other insulators told Jack and Jim about the nail keg 'happening'.

The same lather continued to be a pain in the neck, and at the end of one work day, Langer said, "Hey, fuckface! Did your nails have a strange taste to 'em today?"

As the guy looked at him, Bob said, "You'd better wash out your fucking mouth 'cause I pissed in your nail keg!"

Before heading back to Boston, Bob gave Jack his usual 'do what I say, not what I do' talk.

"Jackie Boy, what's lined up for school next year? And don't even think about telling me you're gonna join the Marine Corps! All you can see are those fucking dress blues. Well, you'll never get a pair of dress blues. All you'll get is some fucking southern redneck running your ass into the ground. And don't think of working full time for your old man either! When it's 120 fucking degrees up in some attic and you're laying fiberglass insulation in the ceiling, you'll learn real fast that you don't want to do it for the rest of your fucking life. It's like shoveling shit against the tide, Jackie Boy … you just never get anywhere!

"Go to college, and with your bullshit and smiling face, you'll end up president of the fucking bank! Say 'hello' to your old man, and don't you dare stop in Danvers for a couple of beers on the way back. I never should've shown you that fucking place.

If you're big enough to sit on the barstool, they'll serve you a shot and a beer!

"Oh, by the way, did you guys hear about those fucking North Koreans? They're just like the Japs … sneaky, slant-eyed cocksuckers. We should just drop 'the bomb' on the whole bunch of them. Maybe it would wipe out all of Korea, and take Japan along with it. Say 'hello' to the guys at The International!"

Chapter 5

The only thing international about the International Pub was that every race known to man would frequent the place. It was a typical 3-D hangout ... dirty, dark, dismal.

Jack summoned up his deepest voice and said to the much-tattooed bartender, "Two beers and a couple of pickled eggs."

The bartender looked at Jack and Jim. "I can't serve you fucking kids. You're not out of kindergarten yet!" He laughed long and hard at his own humor.

Jack smiled 'the smile'. "Oh, we just delivered a load of insulation to Bob Langer up in Maine. He told us to have a couple of cool ones on him at The International, and to give you his best."

"Well, why the fuck didn't you say so? Bobby was the toughest son of a bitch to ever come out of Revere. He musta killed a hundred fucking Japs all by himself. Ya want a draft or a bottle? Two bottles of Pickwick Ale coming up!"

Jim looked at Jack. "Shall we have another one?"

Jack always used Bob Langer's words whenever possible. "Can a bird fly on one fucking wing? Two more Pickwicks and a couple of eggs, please." They laughed as long as the bartender had. This sure as hell beat going to school!

Jim always loved having a few beers. It usually meant that they'd talk about some of the wonderful times they'd had together over the past couple of years. He often called beer 'reminders' because after three or four, you'd always be reminded of something you'd done together. They drained the last beer, and issued a "Take care" to the bartender.

He sounded like Bob Langer as he gave the opinion of a veteran of World War II. "Those slant-eyed bastards are making a move over near Japan, huh? We should drop the fucking bomb on 'em and wipe out the whole fucking country before we start sending guys like you over there to kick ass. Give Bob my best. Take care."

They hopped in the truck and headed back to Newton. Jim pulled up the sleeve of his T-shirt to reveal the tattoo on his left upper arm.

"Ya know, my parents still don't know I've got this tattoo!"

22

Jack, Jim, and Bob Gregg had taken the bus and trolley into Boston. Scolley Square was *the* place to go, and the first stop had to be the Old Howard burlesque show. The sign on the marquee said, "Peaches, Queen of Shake", and that was their first destination. The Old Howard Theatre was pretty well filled up with sailors in their dress whites and old men with crusty suits that had seen better days. The three guys from Newton very seldom, if ever, had the opportunity to actually see a bare tit except in the *National Geographic*, so the Old Howard beat the hell out of daydreaming about jugs!

The vaudeville comedians got the audience laughing with their slapstick acts that most always included a well-endowed woman or two. A seedy-looking announcer would address the onlookers with his carnival pitchman's voice.

"Gentlemen, you're in for a treat like none other! Peaches, Queen of Shake, direct from Hollywood and Las Vegas, where she made grown men cry for more ... or was it less! She deserves a huge welcome from Boston ... let's hear it for Peaches, Queen of Shake!"

It was love at first sight with Peaches and all the other strippers. True, you wouldn't want your sister to be a stripper, but for the girl next door it would be an honorable profession! The three guys would talk for hours about who they'd enjoy seeing bareass. After the 'burley', they roamed around Scolley Square until Jack had another of his great ideas.

Bob Langer had once said, "The only other fucking place that would ever serve you guys is Jack's Lighthouse in Scolley Square."

At that precise moment, they looked across the street at a sign on the second floor. "Jack's Lighthouse". They walked up the stairs and into a bar filled with sailors, all zeroing in on four or five women, who would stop at their tables.

Once again the familiar war cry from the bartender.

"I can't serve you fucking kids! Get the hell out of here!"

Jack looked at him with his 'shocked' look.

"Oh, sir, Bob Langer from Revere said we should stop in after going to the Old Howard."

The bartender answered in a more friendly voice, "I know where the hell Bob is from. How is that crazy bastard?"

He even gave them the first round of 'dimies' free! Dime beers were only about eight ounces, so they downed about six beers as they looked out over Scolley Square. Across the street was a sign lit up. "Ted Liberty, TATTOOS"

Beer tends to warp the brain quickly, especially in sixteen-year-old kids. They walked into Ted Liberty's, and were welcomed by a three-hundred-pound guy with tattoos all over him. The walls were covered with hundreds of pictures of every tattoo you can imagine. They chose the eagle with the American flag, and Jack, Jim, and Bob proceeded to fuck up royally! It hurt like hell to get a tattoo, but the pain couldn't compare with the effect the so-called 'work of art' had on members of their families!

Since the 'art work' was done on the upper left arm, it was concealed even when wearing a T-shirt. Jack went a number of months without his family seeing it. After that period of time, he forgot all about the tattoo. As he was changing his shirt one day, his younger sister Julie walked into his room.

"Jackie has a picture on his arm!" she screamed.

Jack's mother was in shock. "You look like a drunken sailor!"

And Jack's father said very calmly, as he did so often, "Jack, sometimes I just don't understand you!"

His sister Ann, only a year older than he was but a hell of a lot more mature, kind of said it all when she said, "Jackie, I'm afraid Maxine won't think you're so cute anymore! (Maxine was one of her close friends, and Jack always blushed when he saw her!) But, I won't say a word. Just wear long-sleeved shirts!"

"Before we drop the truck off at the garage, let's stop off and see if Chuck Phinney's around. I think he's leaving soon for the Marines," Jim said.

It was hard for Jack to picture Chuck Phinney in the Marine Corps. Many of his capers just didn't quite seem to fit in with Marine Corps tradition.

Chapter 6

Chuck Phinney had just graduated from Tufts College, and was a true genius in many areas. He was an electrical engineer and a mechanical mastermind. He lived next to Bobby Gregg, so Jack and Bobby spent a lot of time with him. Chuck was always working on something out in his garage/workshop. He had worked for a locksmith while going to college, so he frequently put his newfound trade to use.

It was a great adventure to travel with Chuck late at night, unlock the traffic light boxes at major intersections in Newton . . . and change all the lights to red! Chuck also had made a master key for pay telephones … not to steal money, but to make free phone calls. He would open the telephone, hook a string to a lever inside, run the string down through the coin return slot, and close the phone case. Then, he would make a long distance call.

The operator would come on and say, "That will be 75 cents, please."

Chuck would insert 25 cents, pull the string, and the quarter would return. He did that two more times, and the operator would say, "Thank you."

At Tufts, Chuck had a wonderful business, which allowed fellow students to call home all over the country by paying Chuck a small fee!

Chuck's talents were many. He lived on Commonwealth Avenue, just at the start of the "Heartbreak Hills" of the Boston Marathon. Chuck, being ahead of his time, set up microphones on the roof of the house, and would announce some of the runners as they headed up the hills.

"Let's give a big hand to Clarence Demar and send him on his way to a strong finish!"

In the great summer of 1950, Chuck recruited Jack for one of his all time great capers. When driving by the North Station in Boston, Chuck gazed in awe at one of the huge diesel train engines. On the roof of the engine was a huge set of double air horns … one at least six feet long and the other about four feet.

A few days later, Chuck said, "Jack, I need your help. I'm going to confiscate the greatest fucking air horns you've ever seen. They're on a diesel engine at the North Station. All we have to do is take them!"

There was no hemming or hawing with Jack. "For Christ's sake, Chuck! How the hell will we get 'em?"

They each put on a mechanic's 'monkeysuit' like Chuck always wore in his workshop. Chuck brought his toolbox with all the stuff they'd need, and they headed into Boston. They walked into the North Station as if they owned the place, and proceeded out into the train yard where hundreds of trains were headed in and out of Boston. There were maintenance workers everywhere, and no one paid any attention to them.

They climbed up the attached ladder on the diesel engine that led to the horns, and Chuck, in his efficient manner, unbolted the horns. Jack climbed down the ladder, and Chuck handed down the horns. They walked through the station, and headed back to Newton.

Chuck meticulously installed the horns under his 1949 black Ford with just the ends of the horns sticking out under the front bumper. The air tank was under the hood, with a solenoid switch mounted to the steering column. The trial run was one of beauty when many drivers on Route 9 actually thought a train was going to run them off the road!

All Chuck and Jack could say over and over was, "Holy shit!"

In late summer, Chuck was heading off to the Quantico, Virginia, Marine Corps base. He was in the N.R.O.T.C. (Naval

Reserve Officer Training Course) at college, and would serve active duty of two years, then reserve time when leaving active duty. The United States had just entered the Korean War on a small scale, but nobody gave it much thought at the time.

Bob Langer told Jack, "Second Lieutenants are a dime a dozen. Tell your friend Chuck to keep his nose clean and stay clear of the Fleet Marine Force, the ground pounders. If that Korean thing amounts to anything, you know fucking 'A' the Marine Corps will be kicking ass over there. Platoon leaders are nothing but cannon fodder!"

Jack knew that Chuck somehow would work on some angle to stay away from Korea. *Besides*, he thought, *what the hell are we doing over there anyway*?

Chapter 7

The 'endless summer' of 1950 came to a screeching halt after Labor Day when Jack walked into his first class at Huntington Prep School.

He knew the future wasn't bright when the teacher said, "I hope you all had an enjoyable summer, but now it's time to forget the past and buckle down to the task ahead. Open up your minds, and prepare yourselves for a stimulating educational awakening. There will be times that you may question my methods of instilling the delights of learning into your young minds, but I think in the months ahead, you'll learn to appreciate these efforts."

Oh, Jesus, thought Jack, *I'm sure this guy is from the 'Morgenstern School' and will be asking if we jerked off during the summer. I hope I have the balls to tell him, "No, my girlfriend did it for me!"*

Within a week, Jack knew that he and Huntington Prep would have to part company. He would much prefer to be up in that 120-degree attic, and he didn't care what Bob Langer said. The next month or so did nothing to change his mind, and the reports on the expanding Korean situation seemed like the perfect way out of Huntington Prep. It wouldn't be as though he was just quitting – it would be a patriotic move on his part.

American troops were being sent to Korea, and thousands of guys were joining the service. World War II had only been over for five years, and kids who were too young to join during that war were now ready to join in what many of them thought would be an exciting time. For some reason war and the combative side of it always seems glamorous to those who are young and have no idea of what the terror of war really is.

The morning of November 10th, 1950 would sign, seal, and deliver Jack Harrington to the United States Marine Corps. The radio in Jack's room announced the 175th birthday of the Marine Corps with the moving words that had been issued by the commandant of the Corps, General Clifton B. Cates.

"On November 10, 1775, a Corps of Marines was created by a resolution of Continental Congress. Since that date many thousands of men have borne the name Marine. In memory of them it is fitting that we who are Marines should commemorate the birthday of our Corps by calling to mind the glories of its long and illustrious history. During 93 years of the 175 years of its existence the Corps has been in action against the nation's foes.

"From the Battle of Trenton to the Argonne and the Pacific theatre, Marines have won foremost honors in wars, and in the long eras of tranquillity at home, generation after generation of Marines has grown gray in war in every corner of the seven seas that our country and its citizens might enjoy peace and security.

"In every battle and skirmish since the birth of our Corps, Marines have acquitted themselves with the greatest distinction, winning new honors on each occasion until the term 'Marine' has come to signify all that is highest in military efficiency and soldierly virtue.

"This high name of distinction and soldierly repute we who are Marines today have received from those who preceded us in the Corps. With it, we also received from them the eternal spirit which has animated our Corps from generation to generation and has been the distinguishing mark of the Marines in every age.

"So long as that spirit continues to flourish, Marines will be found equal to every emergency in the future as they have been in the past, and the men of our nation will regard us as worthy successors to the long line of illustrious men who have served as 'Soldiers of the Sea' since the founding of the Corps."

The Boston & Worcester bus slowed as it approached the hallowed halls of Huntington Prep.

"I'm going to Park Square today," smiled Jack.

The driver nodded and hit the gas pedal.

Chapter 8

It happened as fast as a Ted Williams drive into the bullpen in right field at Fenway Park. Jack walked the mile over to the Fargo Building, and started the process of joining The United States Marine Corps.

One of the recruiters, who looked like his uniform was ironed on, said in clearly enunciated words, "What makes you think you want to become part of the finest fighting force in the world, or that 'my' Marine Corps will allow you to do that?"

Jack thought quickly back to what Bob Langer once said about Marine Corps boot camp at Parris Island. *"The first word out of your mouth when talking to anyone who isn't a boot had better be 'SIR'!"*

"Sir! A Marine who served in the Pacific works for my father. He told me recently that if I ever decided to serve my country there's no sense being second best. He said I have the makings of a Marine, and if I went into any other branch of service, he'd kick my ass!"

Jack wondered how he came up with that bullshit answer so fast, but could tell the Sergeant liked what he heard when he said, "We may just allow you to wear the 'globe and anchor' sooner than you think! Wait in that line over there!"

As Jack waited in what seemed like endless lines, he wondered how he would tell his parents about leaving Huntington Prep, and heading for Marine boot camp at Parris Island, South Carolina.

George Armanio from Watertown and Steve Charles from New Hampshire were in front and back of Jack in line. George, known as "Greek", and Steve had both read where the Korean War might require the government to draft men into the service. Steve said a Marine recruiter had told him he could probably qualify for tank battalion duty, and Greek wanted to serve with a Marine detachment on board a Navy ship.

Jack didn't tell 'em what Langer had always said, "They'll promise you the fucking world, and you'll end up a ground pounder in the Fleet Marine force!"

They took aptitude tests, medical exams, were asked if they had homosexual tendencies (most of them weren't quite sure what that meant), and if they liked girls. Oh well, at least they weren't asked if masturbation had ever entered their minds! Jack was told he would leave for P.I. on November 17ᵗʰ, 1950, and Greek and Steve had the same orders!

Heading home by way of Scolley Square made a lot of sense to a guy who had just joined the Marine Corps thought Jack as he headed for the Lighthouse that Jim Emery always said was named for him. The stairway up to "Jack's Lighthouse" smelled like a combination of the men's room at Fenway Park and the locker room at Newton High, but the smell of cheap perfume cleared your sinuses real fast as you entered the smoke-filled bar room.

"Hey, Sweetie, I've been waiting all my life for you," purred one of the many hookers hanging around.

Jack smiled and headed straight for the bar.

Ted Liberty blinked his usual welcome across the street as the bartender bellowed, "Hey, any fucking friend of Bobby Langer's gets top shelf treatment! What's new, pal? You joined the fucking Marine Corps? Well, if you're half the fucking Marine Langer was, we can all sleep well at night knowing we're as safe as having Big Ted at the plate with bases loaded!"

In between his hyena-like laughter came the magic words every patron of the pubs dreams of … "You're drinking on me today, pal. The bar is yours!"

The trolley ride to Cleveland Circle and quick bus trip to Newton Center had Jack dreaming of dress blues and heroic deeds. An open bar has a way of doing that to an eighteen-year-old kid who has just joined The Corps!

Jack had a feeling of elation he hadn't experienced before as he walked home. He'd made a decision on his own that would no doubt have a great deal to do with the rest of his life. He wasn't taking someone else's advice, and he wasn't following others down the same old street to mediocrity. He had grabbed the bull by the horns, climbed on his back, and was ready to ride.

Explaining his decision to his parents even had a calming effect on him. After all, it was a great honor to serve in the United States Marine Corps, and he felt they would understand.

At first, his mother thought he was kidding until he explained all the details.

His father said, "Jack, sometimes I just don't understand you, but I'm very proud of you just the same!"

They were both extremely worried, especially his mother, as there was more and more news about American forces heading for Korea to help stop communism from spreading into South Korea.

Bob Langer, in his own down-to-earth way, probably gave Jack the best advice he could get about Parris Island.

"Never fuck with a drill instructor! Just keep your fucking mouth shut, pretend the only words you know are 'Sir! Yes, Sir!' … and, never volunteer! Never let them know that you're tired, scared shitless, or not ready for anything they can hand out. Your first few weeks you'll wonder what the fuck you've done to your life, but believe me, when you leave the Island, you'll be Marine for the rest of your life. I wish to God I was going with you!"

Chapter 9

The train pulled out of South Station and rattled toward Providence, RI, where more recruits would get on board. The clickety-clack of the train wheels put each new marine into a trance, their own thoughts keeping time to the sounds that brought them closer to what was often described as 'hell on earth'.

The conductor droned, "Providence, Providence, Rhode Island," as the station platform appeared.

The waiting recruits boarded the train quickly. A mother tearfully hugged her embarrassed son as all eyes peered out of the Pullman car at him. Jack was glad he had said his goodbyes at home.

Jack's first and only trip to Grand Central Station had been in 1939, with his father to spend a couple of days at the World's Fair. He was more impressed with the huge ceiling of Grand Central than he was of anything at the Fair. The blue sky ceiling, with stars placed as they appeared on a clear night, welcomed him to New York just as they had eleven years before.

The group more than doubled in New York. Any Boston Red Sox fan only knew one thing about New Yorkers … they were the enemy. After all, didn't the Yankees always knock the Sox out of any shot at the World Series?

The sleeper train to Washington, D.C. awaited them as they walked under the indoor sky with the North star shining … hopefully, a good omen. The leader of the new group was a giant of a guy with a Brooklyn accent that echoed through the train like a raspy saxophone played by a kid in the seventh grade band, who should have stuck to the drums.

'Brooklyn' was also a card player who got things rolling on the trip with a poker game. Pints and half pints of liquid courage appeared, and the guzzlers got tougher and tougher. In between relieving each card player of their money, Brooklyn made it real clear to everyone on the train that no one had better ever fuck with him.

"Any D.I. lays a hand on me, I'll break his fucking neck," screamed the big guy.

Jack took Bob Langer's advice. He kept his mouth shut and tried to get some sleep as the train headed south to D.C. and then on to Yemassee, South Carolina.

Yemassee had a population of about three hundred, but looking from the train it seemed that nobody lived there. No station was in sight, only a dilapidated general store and another set of railroad tracks.

Brooklyn moved to a window, and pushed it up to get fresh air into the train. With everyone gawking out the windows, no one noticed the train door open.

A lone Marine in a perfectly fitted shirt, creased trousers, shoes that shined like the Grand Central North star, campaign hat, and swagger stick stood in silence listening to the nervous buzz of raw recruits.

The Marine moved faster than Superman on his best day, and stood erect beside Brooklyn's back.

In guttural, clearly enunciated words he screamed, "YOU FUCKING MAGGOT! WHO TOLD YOU TO OPEN THAT WINDOW?"

The tough guy from Brooklyn stood stunned, speechless.

"YOU SHITBIRD! IF YOU HAVE HEARING PROBLEMS, YOU CAN'T BE IN MY MARINE CORPS! DO YOU HEAR ME, SHIT FOR BRAINS?"

There wasn't a sound on the train. The big guy's lips trembled as he tried to speak. Tears welled up in Brooklyn's eyes as words refused to leave his mouth.

The Marine stood within a few inches of him, and again screamed, "YOU FUCKING PANSY! IF YOU HEAR ME, I WANT THE WORDS 'SIR! YES, SIR!' TO LEAVE YOUR FILTHY MOUTH! DO YOU UNDERSTAND ME?"

Tears flowed as a meek, "Sir! Yes, Sir!" came faintly from within the big guy.

The D.I. screamed, "I CAN'T HEAR YOU, MAGGOT!"

As the Brooklyn tough guy sobbed in a louder voice, 'SIR! YES, SIR!", the D.I. headed for the train door and screamed, "ALL I WANT TO SEE IS ASSHOLES AND ELBOWS! GET OUT ON THE FUCKING TRACKS!"

The stampede was on. Everyone fought to get off the train, lining up along the tracks in shock. No one spoke. Jack knew they all felt the same fear of being torn to pieces by someone in a campaign hat.

A line of trucks, like cattle cars loaded up for the trip to the slaughter house, headed for Parris Island. Hardly a word was spoken during the hour-long trip.

Chapter 10

They unloaded in the eerie darkness on the asphalt parade ground, then filed into the long wooden barracks. Four drill instructors walked up and down the squad bay looking them over. Each had spit-shined shoes with metal taps on the soles. The only noise in the barracks was the tap-dance click of the soles on the floor. Finally, the same-sounding voice they had heard on the train came from a sergeant who stood in the middle of the squad bay.

"I want to give you people some advice. I suggest you listen up since you will be expected to retain everything you're told, the first and only time it's said. That will hold true each and every day that you're here.

"Since 1917, Parris Island has been sending new Marines off the island to serve the Corps proudly all over the world. Some of you may join this elite group. The bedrock of a Marine's character is honor, courage, and commitment. During the days ahead many of you will be weeded out and sent back to civilian life. You won't be allowed to wear the globe and anchor, and in later years will realize you missed out on being a member of the finest fighting fraternity in the world.

"Those of you who advance on schedule will be on this beautiful island retreat for twelve weeks. When you're thinking you're tired, you're mistreated, and you're overworked, remember what was told to me when I was in your place before going to the Pacific to say 'hello' to the Japs."

'Your fellow Marines in combat with you don't want to hear tired. They don't want to hear mistreated. They don't want to hear overworked. They want to hear from a fellow Marine who's ready to kick ass.'

"That's all I have to say, but I know Corporal Harrelson wants to welcome you to Parris Island."

"For the next twelve weeks, the only words we ever want to hear from you are either, 'SIR! NO, SIR!' or 'SIR! YES, SIR!' Do you understand me?"

A faint "Sir! Yes, Sir!" was heard, and the D.I. screamed, "I CAN'T HEAR YOU!"

At that point a loud and clear "SIR! YES, SIR!" was yelled out.

"In a few minutes you will turn in your cigarettes and any pogey bait you may have. Your days of lighting up or eating Baby Ruth bars are over. Do you people understand me?"

"SIR! YES, SIR!"

"From the looks of you idiots, it will be impossible to turn you into members of the finest fighting force known to man. If any of you survive the first two weeks it will be a miracle, but we will then know if you have the balls to stand tall and at least have a slight chance of wearing the globe and anchor.

"You will drop your cocks and grab your socks at 0400 tomorrow, and do so for the next two weeks. After that, if you don't fuck up, it may be at 0500, but I doubt that will ever happen. In the next day or two, you will have time to write home to tell your loved ones you are fine and dandy, and that the United States Marine Corps is treating you well. If you don't think you're being treated well, you can tell it to the chaplain, but God help your asses if you do!

"You will have more physical exams, more shots, and be issued your gear tomorrow. You will shave and shower every day. For those who don't shave yet, you will begin tomorrow. You will be placed in platoons over the next 48 hours, and meet your drill instructors eyeball-to-eyeball. Their main goal in life is to make your fucking life miserable and run your ass into the ground. Every D.I. has his own way of getting a point across to you, so be prepared to shape up or ship the fuck out. However, there are usually only two ways to leave Parris Island ... either by earning the globe and anchor ... or in a fucking box. Do you understand me?"

"SIR! YES, SIR!"

They hit the sack that night at around 2400. Two hours later the lights came on.

"FALL OUT ON THE COMPANY STREET ON THE FUCKING DOUBLE!"

They lined up on the asphalt in their underwear, and the squared away corporal said, "I forgot to tell you fucking idiots one of the most important things for you to remember. Keep in mind at all times that your soul may belong to God, but your ass is ours! Do you people understand me?"

It was a shivery night even for South Carolina standards, but no one dared to even think about shaking as they echoed their answer ... "SIR! YES, SIR!"

Before Jack climbed into the top bunk he whispered to the big guy from Brooklyn, who had the lower bunk, "If that had been me on the train with the D.I. today, I probably would have pissed in my pants!"

No one had spoken to Brooklyn since the incident, and he hadn't said a word to anyone either. He looked at Jack with a sad but relieved look, and whispered back as he extended his huge hand, "Thanks! I'm Carmen Manero."

The lights went out, and Jack Harrington wondered what the hell he had gotten himself into.

Chapter 11

Reality set in for Jack as he stood in line to get his haircut. His hair was cut short anyhow, but the boot camp cut was right to the scalp … not a hair left on his head. It was then that everyone became the same, and maybe the D.I.'s were right.

The six-foot-four-inch corporal, Ladue from Louisiana, called us baldheaded monkeys, but not as smart. Our head D.I., Corporal Philips from Georgia, called us the scum of the earth, and he wanted to puke when he looked at us. The third D.I., Corporal Dugan from Massachusetts, said we were more fucked up than a Chinese fire drill, and he was looking forward to shipping us to a 'slow platoon', which would extend boot camp for at least three more weeks!

Platoon #263 lived in metal Quonset huts that slept 16 men each. Every day they fell out on the Company Street at 0400. The pace of life on Parris Island was set at triple time.

From the moment you awoke until you hit the sack at night, you were in third gear and always ran over the speed limit. You shaved, showered, and emptied your body of the previous day's intake in a matter of minutes. No one ever quite got used to the long toilet-seated troughs where dozens of boots sat side by side each morning.

"When you fucking people are out in the field or hunting for Luke the Gook, you'd welcome sitting on the community shitter. You will always make do with what is available in our Marine Corps. You will be like a fucking chameleon. You will adapt to the situation. Do you understand me?"

"SIR! YES, SIR!"

Everything was scheduled like clockwork ... morning chow, classes in everything from personal hygiene to field stripping an M-1 rifle, map reading, Marine Corps history, etc., with constant sessions of close order drill and physical training. Within a few weeks the platoon started to shape up, and close order drill no longer looked like people fleeing in panic from a burning building.

Near the end of the third week, the platoon scrambled into formation in the darkness of a cold morning in December.

"You fucking people will be allowed to enter the Post Exchange today. You will have the privilege of buying cigarettes, one bar of pogey bait, some writing paper, and stamps. If you don't fuck up, one of these days the smoking lamp will be lit. If any one of you idiots decides a little grab ass is in order while at the PX, the entire platoon will suffer. Do you understand me?"

"SIR! YES, SIR!"

"One other thing. Civilian employees operate the PX. Most of them are women. The only words out of your mouths will be, 'Yes, Ma'am' or 'No, Ma'am'. Do you understand me?"

"SIR! YES, SIR!"

"If any of you Romeo's think a little extra conversation is in order, you'll be explaining your sudden impulse for fraternization to the brig warden. Ten days on piss and punk, that's bread and water, ain't worth whispering sweet nothings to someone you'll never see again. So, keep any of your loving thoughts to yourself. Do you Errol Flynn wannabes understand me?"

"SIR! YES, SIR!"

After noon chow, the long-awaited order of "The smoking lamp is lit" was given as the platoon stood in formation. The familiar D.I. voice rang out.

"You idiots will smoke by the numbers. #1. You put the cigarette in your mouth. #2. You light it. #3. You take a drag. Do you understand me?"

"SIR! YES, SIR!"

"One! Two! Three!"

The first drag wasn't as great as anticipated, but each boot knew the remainder of the cigarette meant they had reached another level in their twelve week tour on the island. Before the second drag was ordered, the D.I., with a surly look of pleasure, gave his next command.

"ALL RIGHT YOU FUCKING MAGGOTS! PUT OUT THOSE SMOKES!"

He then proceeded to demonstrate the fine art of 'field stripping' a cigarette.

"If any of you fuckups ever earn the globe and anchor, which is highly fucking unlikely, wherever you may go in my Marine Corps you will always field strip your butts. You split the cigarette paper, let the tobacco blow away, roll the paper into the size of a small beebee, and put it in your pocket. Do you understand me?"

"SIR! YES, SIR!"

One drag of a cigarette after a three-week wait was like Chinese water torture. The platoon agreed that if they ever had the chance, they'd hang Corporal Ladue by his balls!

Carmen Manero, who had recovered from the fatal day on the train, laughingly told Jack he was keeping his mouth shut, but did hope he ran into Corporal Ladue in New York someday. "He'd look good trying to swim the East River in a cement life jacket!"

Chapter 12

All three D.I.'s were their usual spit and polish, and their manner was as shiny and clean as their double-soled, metal-tapped shoes.

The battalion commander, a captain, was introduced, and gave a 'gung-ho' speech about training in general and what was expected of the platoon in the weeks ahead. He then introduced the chaplain, who spoke of church services and asked if any one had any problems. Each boot remembered, '*If you have any complaints you can tell the chaplain, but God help you if you do!*'

The only sound from Platoon 263 was a loud, "Sir! No, Sir!"

The chaplain went on to say that if anyone wished to be baptized, it would be done the following morning, and would require about a half-day's time out of our busy schedule.

Jack immediately thought, *A half day away from the D.I.'s ... maybe even a cigarette ... maybe even chow at a different mess hall without hearing 'Outside on the fucking double!' five minutes after you sat down with your food! Don't volunteer! Don't volunteer! But, was this volunteering? No, it wasn't!*

When the chaplain said, "Anyone who wishes to be baptized, please speak up", "Sir! Yes, Sir!" flowed from his mouth.

The next morning he headed for the chaplain's office with Greek, who had the same wonderful thoughts Jack had. The half day was spent lounging in the church area to supposedly read over what baptism was all about. What a joyous time! Jack closed his eyes and dreamt of what an eighteen-year-old kid at Parris Island would dream of.

An hour or so later Greek and Jack were baptized, went to the chow hall near the church, and afterwards the smoking lamp was lit. They smoked two each, field stripped them, and laughed hysterically over the wonderful break they had created for themselves.

After evening chow they were ordered to report to the D.I.'s house. The D.I.'s lived in huts, too, but always called wherever they slept their 'house'.

Greek and Jack knocked on the door, and heard, "I can't hear you!"

They knocked harder.

"Get into my fucking house!"

"Sir! Reporting as ordered, Sir!"

The three D.I.'s stared at them as one said, "Have you seen the fucking light you maggots?"

Not knowing what to say, they just yelled, "SIR! YES, SIR!"

Corporal Ladue stood before them, only an inch or two away. He told them that the chaplain's assistant, a corporal, was a friend of his, and had reported to him on their religious experience.

Ladue looked only at Jack and said, "You shitbird! Maybe you're not quite as dumb as we thought. When the chaplain asked if you were being treated well you said yes, and that your D.I.'s were probably the best at Parris Island. A very smart fucking answer you maggot! If your answer had been much different, the only light you'd be seeing would be from the shine of my size twelves as I kicked your ass all over this fucking island. Do you understand me, shit-for-brains?"

"SIR! YES, SIR!"

"Harrington, aren't all Catholics baptized soon after coming into this wonderful world of ours? You're an Irishman, so you must be Catholic. How come they didn't dunk you in the drink when you were a kid?"

"Sir! My family wasn't too active in the church, and I was never told about being baptized when I was a baby. Since I may serve with the Marine Corps in Korea, I wanted to be sure I covered all the bases, Sir!"

"Get out of my house, maggot!"

"Harrington's balls ain't brass quite yet, but it looks like they will be," laughed Ladue. "I liked that 'covered all my bases' bullshit!"

Chapter 13

"Platoon 263! Out on the Company Street! Mail Call!"

Some guys never got any mail **ever**, which had to be devastating to them. Those who did get mail had to 'run the gauntlet'. A D.I. would call out your name. Each boot would run out of ranks and stand at attention in front of the D.I. to receive mail, never knowing what to expect.

"Is this from your girlfriend? Were you fucking her before you joined my Marine Corps? I see lipstick with S.W.A.K. on the back of the envelope, maggot. What the fuck does that mean?"

"Sir! Sealed with a kiss, Sir!"

"Were those lips ever around your pecker, maggot?"

"Sir! No, Sir!"

"Well, I bet they're around someone's now! Out of my sight, idiot! Harrington, you have a fucking package! Come to our house when the platoon is dismissed!"

"Sir! Reporting as ordered, Sir!"

"Who the fuck is this package from?"

"Sir! My mother, Sir!"

"You aren't supposed to receive packages, shitbird! Open it up!"

There, wrapped carefully, were homemade brownies. As Jack stood at attention, he heard, "You, of course, wish to share these with the finest drill instructors on Parris Island, don't you?"

"Sir! Yes, Sir!"

As Jack continued to stand at attention, with tears welling up in his eyes, the D.I.'s ate all but one brownie.

"Do you want this brownie, maggot, or should we give it to the chaplain's assistant from you?" Unable to speak for a moment, he heard, "We don't hear you!"

"Sir! Give it to the chaplain's assistant, Sir!"

"Get the fuck out of our sight!"

"Sir! Yes, Sir!"

"Oh, Harrington, we wanted to check out your package just to cover all the bases."

Dear Mom,

Thanks for the brownies. They were great. Please don't send any more packages though. There are too many guys to try and share things with, and I don't want to leave anyone out. The food is good here, but I sure miss your meatloaf. I'll be home soon.

> *Love to you, Dad, Ann, and Julie,*
>
> *Jack*

Chapter 14

"You're a long way from being presented with the globe and anchor emblem. You've been here for seven weeks, and, as we told you from the start, Platoon 263 will be an honor platoon no matter what. Tomorrow at 0600, we will head for the rifle range with full packs. There will be no fucking stragglers. When you are in Korea killing gooks, you'll find out real fast that stragglers don't make it!

"Every Marine is basically a rifleman. You will qualify with the M-1 rifle every year no matter what your job is in this Marine Corps. To put one grunt eyeball-to-eyeball with the enemy in a combat situation takes another dozen Marines with other responsibilities. If combat casualties are too high, some of those non-combat Marines will be called in to do the grunt's work. You may be a clerk-typist with the division, a band member, a cook, or a Hollywood Marine in California and be called upon to squeeze off some rounds at live targets. Therefore, you will be ready! All Marines are riflemen! Do you understand me?"

"Sir! Yes, Sir!"

"You've learned to field strip your weapons blindfolded and put them back together. You will now learn how to fire your weapons. You'll be squeezing off rounds at targets from 200 to 500 yards away. You will make every shot count, as the day will come when your fellow Marines will need you. Do you understand me?"

"Sir! Yes, Sir!"

As they moved out toward the rifle range, the echo of small arms fire got louder and louder.

The D.I.'s yelled, "Close it up, you fucking idiots!"

Living at the rifle range for two weeks was like going from a two-buck flophouse to The Ritz in Boston. Well, not quite, but a two-story barracks building was a welcome change. The entire platoon was in one big squad bay, with the D.I.'s 'house' right outside the swinging doors to the squad bay.

The first week at the range was spent on mess duty and classes on different weapons. Jack and Greek lucked out and were sent to the 'spud locker' for mess duty. The spud locker was a small, separate building where hundreds of pounds of potatoes were peeled and sent over to the mess hall. Cabbage heads were also cut up for coleslaw and delivered to the mess hall.

Only two guys worked at the locker, so every once in a while one guy could sneak a cigarette while the other watched for any D.I.'s. It was a great job, and Jack and Greek thought maybe they got the job because of what they had told the chaplain. Jack also had a passing thought about the brownies. Maybe they felt bad about his not getting any!

Corporal Dugan appeared in the squad bay, and everyone snapped to attention.

"Did you shitbirds see some idiot boots in formation with rolls of shit paper around their necks?"

"Sir! Yes, Sir!"

"Well, those maggots didn't qualify at the range. If you score over 220 points out of a possible 250, you qualify as an expert rifleman. From 210 to 219, sharpshooter, and from 190 to 210, marksman. You're sucking hind tit with anything under 190 points. Those pussies wearing shit paper are non-qualifiers!

"And, for you fucking geniuses who figure you'll never be assigned to the Fleet Marine Force if you don't qualify, think again! You'll have the same chance of being a ground pounder as a high expert does. My Marine Corps doesn't discriminate when it comes to the opportunity of getting your ass shot off! Do you understand me?"

"Sir! Yes, Sir!"

"Pay close fucking attention to the 'snapping in' exercises you'll be receiving for the next two days. You will learn the standing, sitting, kneeling, and prone positions. You will spend hours working on these positions. The only difference when you qualify and have practice runs is that you'll be using live ammo!"

"Harrington, what did our beloved commandant, General Vandegrift, say about our duty to use our weapons in the proper manner?"

"Sir! The commandant said, 'Be alert, and when the enemy appears, shoot calmly, shoot fast, and shoot straight!' Sir!"

"On my command, you will all repeat the creed of a United States Marine regarding his rifle. You will speak loud and clear, do you understand me?"

"Sir! Yes, Sir!"

"Speak, you fucking maggots!"

"Sir! This is my rifle. There are many like it, but this one is mine.

My rifle is my best friend. It is my life. I must master it as I must master my life.

My rifle without me is useless. Without my rifle, I am useless. I must fire my rifle true. I must shoot straighter than my enemy who is trying to kill me. I must shoot him before he shoots me. I will . . .

My rifle and myself know that what counts in this war is not the rounds we fire, the noise of our burst, nor the smoke we make. We know that it is the hits that count. We will hit . . .

My rifle is human, even as I, because it is my life. Thus, I will learn it as a brother. I will learn its weaknesses, its strength, its parts, its accessories, its sights, and its barrel. I will ever guard it against the ravages of weather and damage. I will keep my rifle clean and ready, even as I am clean and ready. We will become part of each other. We will . . .

Before God I swear this creed. My rifle and myself are the defenders of my country. We are the masters of our enemy. We are the saviors of my life.

So be it, until victory is America's and there is no enemy, but Peace!

Sir!"

Chapter 15

One of the guys on mess duty was able to confiscate a small container of strawberry jam from the mess hall, and Greek appeared in the spud locker with it. It was Jack's job to somehow get some bread to go along with the jam.

After noon chow, he put three slices of bread in his hat and left the mess hall, heading to the privacy of the spud locker. Cpl. Dugan approached him on the way, and noticed his hat sitting in a strange position.

"Take off your cover, idiot!"

Jack froze as he heard, "Did you hear me, shit for brains?"

"Sir! Yes, Sir!"

He took off the cover and the slices of bread fell to the sidewalk.

"What are you doing? Feeding the fucking birds, Harrington?"

Jack stammered as the D.I. rolled the bread into a ball and tossed it up and down like a baseball.

"After your spud locker duty, report to my house, fuck up!"

Later, the three D.I.'s proceeded to chew Harrington a new asshole, and then handed him a bucket of water and a toothbrush. For the next six hours he scrubbed the long wooden deck in the hallway opposite the squad bay.

"If, for some strange fucking reason, you ever leave this island, Harrington, we're going to recommend you for food service duty. You can become a baker, and have all the fucking bread you'll ever want!"

The following morning the time had come for the platoon to put into action what they had learned over the past few weeks.

"Everything you are ever ordered to do in this Marine Corps is to insure success in combat. Today is the day you fire your rifle for qualification and, as you fuckers know, every Marine is basically a rifleman. So, a little advice for you.

"Don't hurry your shots, but don't stand around with your finger up your ass either. Caress that trigger housing as if it was your girlfriend's tit! When you do that, you're always hoping to get to the promised land. Well, when you gently squeeze off a round, the promised land isn't some warm pussy . . . it's the chest of some fucking gook who's trying to kill you! If you jerk the trigger and miss your intended target, Luke the Gook won't give you a second chance! He'll pump a round right between your horns! Do you understand me?"

"Sir! Yes, Sir!"

From the first time Jack fired a round with the M-1 rifle, he was an absolute natural. The day before qualification day, he shot a 238 out of a possible 250, for one of the highest rounds ever by a boot. The wind changed drastically on qualification day, but he still managed to shoot high expert – 228.

Cpl. Dugan said, "Harrington, you weren't feeding the fucking birds today, but if you had any thoughts of being a fucking office pinky you can kiss them goodbye. My Marine Corps doesn't want a 228 shooter pounding a fucking typewriter in H&S Company. Becoming a Marine Corps baker is out of the question, too! Since you can hit a twenty-inch bullseye at 500 yards, you'll be squeezing off rounds at Luke the Gook before you know it! Are you ready for live fucking targets, Harrington?"

"Sir! Yes, Sir!"

The march back to main side from the rifle range meant that Platoon 263 was on the downhill run. They were feeling very 'salty' since their hair had grown out a quarter of an inch or so, and they even had to get a skin-close trim on the sides. This meant they were only a few weeks away from leaving Parris Island!

Chapter 16

"At ease! The smoking lamp is lit!"

The three D.I.'s stood in front of Platoon 263 and announced the final week's schedule.

"When you maggots arrived here eleven weeks ago, we were positive that recruiters around the country had their head up their ass when thinking you had any chance to make it through Parris Island. You looked like monkeys trying to fuck a football!

"Unless you fuck up during the next five days, it looks like you not only will receive the globe and anchor and your P.F.C. stripe, but you have a good shot at honor platoon. We are here to remind you that your ass is still ours, and if Platoon 263 doesn't make honor platoon, the shit will hit the fan! Do you understand me?"

"Sir! Yes, Sir!"

"We will have a full inspection of all your gear at 0700 tomorrow by the battalion inspection team. The inspection includes your living quarters, your locker boxes, and your weapon. You will be under the gun to answer any questions directed at you. The day after tomorrow, you will be required to go through close order drill in front of a judging team on the parade ground. If all goes well, you will be receiving your orders as to where your next duty station will be at the end of this week.

"You are now in the same situation you faced in the back seat of your automobile with your girlfriend. You kissed her, you got bold and felt her tits, and you finally thought you'd reach the promised land. Well, you haven't reached the promised land yet, and we're here to tell you ... don't fuck up or you'll strike out just like you probably did with your girlfriend! Do you understand me?"

"Sir! Yes, Sir!"

The company, including Platoon 263, passed in review while the band played the Marine Corps Hymn. If that doesn't give you that tingling feeling in your spine and make you stand a little taller, **nothing** will! The thought flashed through Jack's mind that he had survived the worst twelve weeks of his life, and he was extremely proud of himself! Then, practically before the sound of the band left his ears, he was in formation for a final conflict with the D.I.'s!

"You are no longer maggots, idiots, and fuck ups! You are leaving here as members of an honor platoon and the United States Marines. We wish you well in your future assignments, especially those of you who end up serving in Korea. Keep your weapon clean, always carry a pair of clean socks, and field strip those fucking cigarettes! Welcome to our Marine Corps! Semper Fi!"

The buses were waiting to take new Marines to the airport or train station in Charleston. Each man loaded his seabag onto the bus as the D.I.'s said a word or two to each man.

"Harrington," said Cpl. Dugan as he shook Jack's hand, "be sure and thank your mother for the brownies, and maybe she'll bake you some bread!"

No other words were called for. They each smiled as Jack got on the bus!

Chapter 17

Jack sat beside Carmen Manero on the flight to La Guardia airport in New York. It was his first flight, and he asked Carmen if he'd ever flown before.

"Yeah, I fly to Vegas a couple of times a month. It's a piece of cake, but don't try and open the window!"

They both laughed, and then Jack asked why Carmen had joined the Marine Corps.

"Some of my friends joined the Marine Corps Reserve, and I signed up just for the hell of it. A year ago nobody thought there'd ever be any reason to call reserves to active duty. The Korean deal changed all that, and my group was called in. I could have gotten out of it, but decided I'd stick with it."

"How the hell could you have gotten out of being called in?"

"It's who you know, and what favors they owe you in this world, Jack. Let's just say I'm well connected in New York, and at the snap of two fucking fingers I'd be a civilian if I wanted to be."

"Yeah, Carmen, but then you'd be worried about being drafted. They're beginning to draft people like they did in World War II."

Carmen, imitating the D.I. on the train, answered, "You fucking maggot! Do you have hearing problems? I told you it's not what the fuck you know, but **who** you know. One phone call to the right person, and I'd be classified as 4-F in the draft. But, as I said, I'll do my time just like you and the other shitbirds from our platoon!"

At La Guardia at least two dozen people were waiting to greet Carmen Manero. His mother and girlfriend wore long fur coats that shone as brightly as Marine Corps shoes, and all the men wore camel's hair coats and fedoras with the brim turned down. Everyone hugged Carmen, and he introduced Jack to his mother, father, and girlfriend.

A Ted Liberty lookalike peered right through Jack as he said, "I'll bet no fucking drill sergeants fucked with Carmen!" as the others mumbled, "Yeah, yeah".

Jack spoke in his best authoritative Marine voice.

78

"Sir, Carmen was the leader of our platoon, and commanded great respect from our drill instructors. He was the only one they never intimidated!"

Before Jack headed for his Boston connection the bear hug from Carmen said it all, but just for good measure he said, "You always have a home away from home in Brooklyn. If I don't see you in our Marine travels, call me. The Little Italy Restaurant will put you in touch with me. And remember, ... if you ever need anything, let me know!"

Walking to his plane, all Jack could think of were the pictures he had once seen of Al Capone and his Chicago cronies. Whatever Carmen was or did made no difference to Jack. Carmen had been stripped bare by the D.I. in the train, yet he took it in stride and never made excuses. He made it through Parris Island with flying colors, and that was good enough for Jack.

Hopefully, he and Carmen would meet again.

Chapter 18

As the thwack, thwack of the chopper blades stopped on the deck of the *Repose*, Jack awoke with a jerk and didn't know where he was.

A Navy corpsman quickly brought him back to the present time.

"This ain't as good as liberty in Chicago, gyrene, and you probably won't get laid, but it beats fucking around with Luke the gook. We'll put you back in never-never land with more syringe magic, take out the pieces of fine Chinese jewelry Luke gave you, and you'll have the run of this cruise ship. Nothing is too good for you jungle bunnies, and we'll make Florence Nightingale's bedside manner seem like thirty days in the brig on piss and punk!"

To Jack and other Marines, the *Repose* was as if they had been given carte blanche at *The Ritz Carleton* in Boston, with a penthouse overlooking Boston Public Gardens and the swan boats!

Although this was a floating hospital, it was like Mass General Hospital or any other great medical center. It was immaculate, and all the Navy personnel had one thing in mind. Give the Marines the best care possible . . . and they did!

Jack was cleaned up, and taken into the operating room to remove the shrapnel from both wounds. It wasn't quite the piece of cake Jack thought it would be, as he had to receive four pints of blood during the operation. When he came out of the anesthesia, he was in the cleanest of clean beds. He knew exactly how lucky he was to be there, and not with the graves registration people in Korea.

General Pollack, the outgoing commanding general of the 1st Division, was scheduled to tour the hospital ship and personally present Purple Hearts to the Marines. The general came aboard with the usual entourage following him ... a few enlisted men and a 1st lieutenant, who was his aide.

There was a Marine two beds away from Jack, who had been hit very badly in the arm and had lost an eye.

The general stopped at his bedside to present the Purple Heart and, trying to cheer the Marine up, in gung-ho fashion said, "We'll have you back on line in no time at all, Marine!"

The wounded Marine looked at the general and said with a smile, "In a pig's ass you will, General!"

Everyone with the general froze, and there wasn't a sound from anyone.

Then, the general cleared his throat, and said laughingly, "You're all Marine, son! Good luck to you!"

He touched the young Marine on the shoulder as the subordinates breathed a sigh of relief and laughed nervously!

At Jack's bed, the general said, "Corporal, I won't tell you that you'll be back on line soon because I see this is your third Purple Heart. With three Purple Hearts, we don't send anyone back to the line. We don't want to push your luck! Does that meet with your approval, Corporal?" he said with a smile.

"Sir! Yes, Sir!"

"Good work, and good luck to you, son!"

In the next couple of days, Jack hobbled through some of the wards on the ship, and then realized more than ever how lucky he was. So many Marines had missing limbs and other wounds that would drastically change their life. He thought of Bill Dean Boyer and all the other Marines he knew that had been killed. Being on the hospital ship, no matter in what condition, would be welcome to them. Jack wiped his eyes, and went back to his ward.

In the pit of his stomach he had that nervous ache that told him that no matter what the general said, he'd be sent back to the MLR. However, the hospital ship was filled over capacity, and was scheduled to sail to Yokosuka, Japan and transfer all the patients to the naval hospital there. They arranged to transfer some extra patients from the *U.S.S. Hope* over to the *Repose* for the trip to Japan.

It was a welcome sight for Jack when he saw Beebop Harris's smiling face, and heard, "Japan will beat the shit out of that fucking New York whore house in Seoul! I knew those mother fuckers wouldn't kill your ass!"

Beebop would have a much longer recuperation period than Jack, but as he said, "Recuperation beats the shit out of visiting that fucking Digger O'Dell in graves registration!"

The short trip to Japan would be both happy and sad. Knowing you had beaten the odds was one thing, but thinking about those who had rolled the dice and lost was a constant in his mind. The light roll of the ship and the little pink pills once again sent Jack backpedaling into a dream world.

Chapter 19

Ten days leave before heading for Camp Lejeune, North Carolina, passed in a flash. Jack's family and friends couldn't believe what they saw. When he left for Parris Island, he weighed 139 pounds, and weighed close to 160 twelve weeks later. He could run the two miles to Bobby Gregg's house without even breathing hard, and as Bob Langer said, "You look like a lean, mean, fighting machine!"

Jack's only mishap on his stay at home was when he asked his sister, Ann, to "Pass the fucking butter" at his first family dinner. The blame for that blunder was placed on the Marine Corps by his mother, and they had brownies and ice cream for dessert!

A call to the Anderson's to see how Carol was doing at college brought a wonderful surprise. Carol answered the phone.

"I'm home for a long weekend for my sister's wedding. This is perfect, Jack. Please be my date for the wedding. I'm so glad you're home. I miss you!"

If only I had a set of dress blues! thought Jack, but the Marine green uniform would surely do. Carol looked like a movie star with her pink maid of honor dress on, and together they were the hit of the wedding.

As the band played the Vaughn Monroe hit 'Racing with the Moon', Carol whispered the plan for the evening.

"I'm driving my sister and Donnie to the airport for their flight to Bermuda. Come with me, and we'll head for the Cape afterwards."

The same cottage that was packed with kids for the graduation party was cold and empty. The setting reminded Jack of a movie. It just seemed too perfect. They turned on the heat and lit a fire in the fireplace. The flames seemed to keep time to Patti Page singing 'Old Cape Cod', and for the first time since boarding the southbound train Jack was completely at ease.

Time spent with Carol in the past was hurried, and always seemed to be in a state of emergency. Perhaps, just as Jack had learned a lot about himself in the last three months, Carol had the same awakening. They weren't just two kids making out. All of a sudden they really cared for each other.

Everything seemed as though it was in slow motion. Wrapped in blankets and pillows by the fire, their unhurried movements turned into the soundest sleep they may have ever enjoyed.

They had breakfast in Sandwich before crossing the Sagamore Bridge and leaving the Cape. The breakfast conversation wasn't one you'd hear from flighty high school kids. It came from the hearts of two people who would have a strong bond forever.

"Jack, I know you have uncertain times ahead of you … exciting, but also scary in many ways. I know we'll see each other again, but who knows when. As we each go our own way, it's important for both of us to remember how much we care for each other. Please be careful, and always know that I love you."

At almost a whisper and holding back tears, Jack told Carol that the short time they had together was something that would stay with him forever. In fairness to both of them, they should concentrate on their commitments, but at some time they would be together again.

They left the small diner hand-in-hand, both knowing that something very special had happened to them.

Chapter 20

Camp Lejeune was the home of the Second Marine Division, Fleet Marine Force. Jack's orders were to report to the 1st Battalion, 6th Marine Regiment for assignment.

It was there that he met an officer from the Boston area who was as tough as they come and one of the great officers in the Marine Corps. Lt. Peter Trimble was a highly decorated veteran of World War II and served in the Pacific with the Marine Corps. After the war he was in the Marine Corps Reserve, and was called back to active duty when the Korean War started.

The lieutenant was tall and thin with an overly square jaw that gave him the Dick Tracy look, only the reddish-brown crew cut replaced the hat Tracy always wore. However, his eyes told the story. They very seldom blinked, and they radiated the belief that he could read your mind. He'd see through you just like Superman enjoyed doing when looking at Lois Lane.

So don't bother to bullshit Lt. Trimble! thought Jack.

He was the intelligence officer for the 1st Battalion, 6th Marines, and wanted a handpicked group of ten men to make up the S-2 section. Duties would require supporting the infantry companies as forward observers, scouts, leading companies on compass marches, doing reconnaissance work, running patrols into enemy territory, etc. Jack Harrington's name was picked from a list of Marines who had done well on aptitude tests and had qualified as an expert rifleman.

In interviewing Harrington, Lt. Trimble explained what the S-2 section was all about and also talked briefly about the Boston area.

"Private Harrington, my job is to prepare the troops under my command for combat. I intend to do that, and I never take the easy road! Combat isn't fun and games, and my training methods aren't either! I have a feeling you're the kind of man I'm looking for to join our section. I can promise you long hours, hard work, and I, personally, will run your ass into the ground! Your reward will be to be part of an elite group, and if you go to Korea, which you eventually probably will, it will stand you in good stead. Do you want to think about your decision, or are you prepared to declare your intentions now?"

Jack thought about *'Don't ever volunteer for anything!'* but, he had this immediate, strong feeling for Lt. Trimble's approach, and felt joining him was the thing to do.

"Sir, I'm prepared to declare my intentions now, and consider it an honor to join your section."

"That's what I like," said the lieutenant, "A man that doesn't beat around the bush! Sgt. Diaz will fill you in on moving your gear. I'm pleased you're joining us. We need a man with a Boston accent!"

Jack moved into a section of the squad bay where the S-2 people would be. So far there were only four members of the group, plus Sgt. Diaz. Sgt. Diaz was also a reserve called back to active duty. He had seen action in the Pacific, and he and Lt. Trimble were dedicated to running the S-2 men into the ground!

The S-2 section wasn't fully staffed yet, but Lt. Trimble showed his true colors when he and Sgt. Diaz had them out on the Company Street at 0500 to do a quick five miles before morning chow! Falling out without weapons was a mistake, and they were ordered to get cartridge belts with bayonet and canteen attached and M-1 rifles.

Lt. Trimble announced, "In combat situations, you always have your weapon at the ready. Your M-1 is a part of you! Never fall out for our little social gatherings without your weapon! We'll do five at 'high port' and sweat out some of that lousy 3.2 beer you drank last night!"

They found out real fast that Lt. Trimble was always out in front of the section. He always wore his cartridge belt with his 45-caliber pistol at his side and his M-2 carbine at high port. He never let up on them or on himself, and even though S-2 bitched and moaned, they were proud to be building a reputation as "those lunatics that run everywhere!"

Chapter 21

After battalion inspection on Saturday, unless a Marine had fire watch or some other duty, he was free to check out his liberty card and leave the base if he wanted to. The squad bay was full of Marines getting ready for liberty when the duty N.C.O. approached Jack with word that a Lt. Phinney had requested his presence in the duty N.C.O. office.

Jack was shocked as he headed down the hall! There was Chuck Phinney, with his second lieutenant bars shining like diamonds.

"Sir! Reporting as ordered, Sir!"

"At ease, Private!" said Chuck in a very military manner. "Please join me on the Company Street!"

Chuck spoke in almost a whisper. "What the fuck are you doing in the F.M.F., you asshole? Don't you know there are much better jobs in the Marine Corps than crawling around the boondocks playing war and maybe going to Korea to get your ass shot off? I'll be back in an hour with civilian clothes on. You put on your 'civies', too, and be neat! We may go to the Officer's Club!"

Jack was speechless as he went back into the barracks to change clothes. In an hour, there was Chuck in a 1949 Oldsmobile 88 to pick him up. After greeting each other without worrying about an audience, Chuck headed for the Officer's Club. Jack was game for a lot of things, but told Chuck his going to the Club was insane.

Chuck answered, "For Christ's sake! If we can walk through the North Station, climb up on a diesel engine and unbolt six-foot air horns, we can do anything!"

They both laughed as Jack realized it was just another crazy challenge for Chuck. Neither one of them gave any thought to the possible ramifications of a Marine officer hanging around with an enlisted man and bringing him to the Officer's Club posing as an officer!

'The Club' was like a high-class country club, and in the lobby at a desk was a corporal greeting the members.

"Good afternoon, Lieutenant Phinney".

"Good afternoon, Corporal. I have a guest that came down from Cherry Point for the day."

"Good afternoon, Sir. Welcome to Camp Lejeune! May I register your name, Sir?"

Without skipping a beat, Jack said, "Good afternoon, Corporal. Lt. Earnshaw, Lt. George Earnshaw is my name. I'm stationed up at Cherry Point."

The bar/lounge was plush and comfortable, and drinks and beers were cheap as hell. Jack thought he had died and gone to Heaven! Over the next few months Chuck and Jack visited 'The Club' fairly often, and all went well until the day Jack, feeling invincible, went alone! Chuck had gone to D.C. for the weekend, and on Saturday afternoon Jack headed over there on his own.

The corporal on duty recognized him, and his "Good afternoon, Lt. Earnshaw!" led to friendly conversation before Jack headed for the lounge. He ordered a beer and drank it leisurely while eating peanuts at the bar. As he turned to look around, there at a table in the corner was Major O'Donnell, the executive officer of the 1st Battalion, 6th Marines.

A few weeks before, the major had personally met members of the S-2 section as Lt. Trimble filled him in on what their responsibilities would be in the upcoming maneuvers at Little Creek, Virginia. For a flash their eyes locked, then Jack turned the other way quicker than you'd snap to attention when an officer appears!

His heart was beating like the time the D.I. asked if he was feeding the fucking birds, but he didn't panic. After slowly finishing the beer, he left from the opposite end of the bar and headed back to have a couple of beers with the other lowly privates at the 'slopchute.'

The following Saturday at battalion inspection, Major O'Donnell appeared with a lieutenant and a couple of N.C.O.'s with clipboards to take notes if need be. He slowly walked through the ranks. If he stopped in front of you, you immediately brought your rifle to port arms and opened the bolt for him to inspect your rifle if he wanted to. He stopped directly in front of Jack Harrington, inspected the rifle, and then moved an inch or two … a whisper away from Jack's face.

"If I ever see you in the Officer's Club again, I will personally run your ass up with the flag in the morning! Do you understand me?"

"Sir! Yes, Sir!"

After inspection, Jack was a basket case. Why hadn't Major O'Donnell disciplined him or had him court-martialed for impersonating an officer?

He would never find out, but he would forever be grateful to the major!

Chapter 22

Do real Marines get the measles? Well, two weeks before the battalion moved out for Little Creek, VA, Jack Harrington looked like the red-checkered tablecloth at the only Italian restaurant in Jacksonville … maybe the only Italian restaurant in all of North Carolina!

He was checked into the base hospital, and when they finally released him, the troops were on their way to maneuvers in Little Creek. Jack reported in to the Sargent Major's office, and was told a couple of dozen men were reporting for duty with the battalion after their ten-day boot leave. He was put in charge of the 'boots' until the troops returned from fun and games in Little Creek.

Looking over the list of incoming Parris Island boots, Jack was shocked to see the name Albert Garbetti, Newton, Massachusetts, listed. Jack knew Big Al from high school, but not real well. He was as big as Carmen Manero, and had hands the size of a shovel. During his jock days in high school, a football looked like an egg sitting in his huge right hand, and when he tackled an opponent it sounded like a belly flop off the ten-foot board at the lake.

Big Al was a star football player, but best remembered by his team mates for putting the sadistic, loud-mouthed football coach out of commission for the season. During a scrimmage he accidentally on purpose crashed into the roly-poly coach, and broke his leg. His "Sorry, Coach. I didn't see ya!" became the catch phrase of the year, and appeared beside his photo in the yearbook!

The new men, including Garbetti, checked in for duty and were told to stand by in the squad bay until 1700 hours for further orders. Jack opened the squad bay swinging door.

"Private Garbetti! Report to the duty N.C.O. office on the double!"

Then, Jack ran back to the office area. Beforehand, he had arranged with another guy to greet Garbetti.

Big Al, in perfect Parris Island form bellowed, "Private Garbetti reporting as ordered, Sir!"

"Stand at ease!" ordered the Marine that Jack had recruited to help him. "Captain Morgenstern will be back in a few minutes."

Al was numb when he heard the name Morgenstern. All he could think of was Newton High School, and the guidance counselor who always asked if you jerked off! The door opened.

Jack's cohort yelled, "Attention!" as Garbetti's six-foot-three inch frame froze at attention.

Jack talked as he entered the room and walked toward the desk, which faced Big Al.

"Don't worry, I'm not going to ask you if you pull your pudd. It's obvious you don't because you'd be short and bald!"

There was silence for a few seconds until Jack and Al were eyeball-to-eyeball, and then uncontrollable laughter filled the room.

Through the laughter Big Al yelled, "You son of a bitch! You scared the shit out of me!"

They went over to the slopchute and drank beers for a couple of hours. Jack recruited Al for the small group known as 'Trimble's Raiders'.

"When the lieutenant gets back, I'll talk to him. We need a guy like you!" Jack told Al.

The stage was set for the Harrington/Garbetti long-run drama. It was well worth the price of admission!

After Garbetti's first week with Lt. Trimble he moaned to Jack, "With friends like you, who needs enemies? Trimble is worse than my fucking D.I.'s!"

They laughed as they downed a beer at the slopchute. The following night they headed for 'J'ville' to have their dress shoes double-soled and taps put on. That done, they went to one of the fifty or so watering holes in town.

Chick Evans was with them. Chick was the map reading expert of the section, and a genius at working out the co-ordinates for all the night compass marches they did in the boondocks of Lejeune. He was from Kentucky, and stated that he was going across the street to the tattoo shop to get a Marine Corps emblem on his arm just like his brother.

Jack and Al said, "What the hell!"

They all had the emblem tattooed on their upper right arm. As the pain of the needle brought tears to his eyes, Jack could hear his mother saying, "You look like a drunken sailor!" and his father saying, "Jack, sometimes I just don't understand you!" Dating Maxine would be out of the question!

At 0500 the following morning, in the shower with a hangover, Jack felt the bandage wrapped around his arm and thought, *Jesus Christ! What the hell is the matter with me?*

The next week they headed out into the field again for five days of nonstop running, compass marches at night, and crawling through the boondocks eating dirt. At around 1600 they prepared a command post for the night, and got ready to chomp down on some C-rations for chow. They were near the crossroads of two dirt roads, and out of nowhere appeared a Studebaker automobile!

Lt. Trimble went over to the car, and returned with two cases of ice-cold beer.

"I'm spending the night with my family. I'll see you at 0500!"

He then left with his wife at the wheel. They figured he had shown his wife on the map where the roads crossed, and, perhaps, had driven out with her a few days earlier to be sure she didn't have a problem finding the spot.

Even though Lt. Trimble was a ball buster, they had great respect for him, but those cold beers delivered in the wilderness of Camp Lejeune would stick in their minds forever! When he returned in the morning, the two empty cases were put in the car, and the lieutenant once again ran them into the ground as if nothing had happened!

Chapter 23

The weeklong maneuvers in the boondocks of Camp Lejeune were always a grueling time. During these training exercises there were always nightlong compass marches. The march might cover four or five miles with five checkpoints involved. Each company was assigned one of Lt. Kimball's S-2 scouts to lead the troops through each leg of the march. Harrington was assigned to Charlie Company, and as he headed out in front of the company commander he once again hoped luck was on his side.

It was pouring rain, and Jack was sure he had fucked up and misread the map, as well as the compass readings. On the fourth leg they had to cross a swamp and then head for the final checkpoint. Fearful of being lost, his heart was pounding for over an hour when suddenly they came out of the woods and were exactly where they were supposed to be!

The company commander, a captain, said, "One hell of a job, Harrington!"

Jack replied, "Thank you, Sir. I was sure we were on track all the way!"

Garbetti had the same sinking feeling with Dog Company. He, too, after hours of zigzagging in the boondocks was sure he was in deep shit. When he came out at the final checkpoint right on course, he breathed a sigh of relief as he, too, was congratulated on the accuracy of the march.

All the troops had been transported by truck out into the boondocks of Lejeune for the exercises. The battalion saddled up for the return to mainside in great spirits. After five nights in the field, thoughts of real showers and a few beers on the horizon had the Marines ready to go as the trucks appeared. Lt. Trimble had announced earlier that the S-2 section would force march back to the base with full packs and show the battalion what real Marines were made of.

Four hours later, the lieutenant led the section into the battalion area on the double. They all had a feeling of great pride as they were dismissed at the barracks, even though a few hours before they had bitched and moaned as the trucks passed them by. Before falling out, Lt. Trimble ordered Harrington and Garbetti to report to him at 0700 the following morning.

Before entering his office, Garbetti gave Harrington a glare as he wondered aloud, "What the fuck does this maniac want from us now? Why did I ever listen to you?"

"The regimental track meet is in two weeks. I want our section to be represented in the meet. Harrington, I want you to run the mile, and, Garbetti, you will enter the shot-put competition," stated the lieutenant.

Jack and Al knew all about the track meet, as they had noticed many of the participants working out getting ready for the competitions. Most of them had been involved in track and field in high school or college, but Jack and Al had never given a thought to entering since they had never had any experience in track and field.

"Garbetti you're big enough to throw that sixteen-pound shot further than most, and since one of the officers was a shot-putter in college, he'll give you some tips. Harrington, I ran track at Colgate and will give you some pointers," said Trimble. "However, most athletes are too wrapped up in form and strategy. It's basically simple … you throw the shot as far as you can, and you run the mile as fast as you can!"

Half the battalion turned out for the meet. The stands were packed and the quarter-mile cinder track was surrounded by Marine Corps flags. As the participants warmed up for the mile, Jack couldn't help but feel like he was going to be run into the ground by these guys. He had been told three of the runners ran the mile for their college teams, and most were runners of the mile in high school.

Lt. Trimble approached Jack just before the race.

"Harrington, most of these guys have all kinds of strategy … start slow, start fast, pick up in the second and third lap, save yourself for the final quarter mile. You have no strategy! Do you understand me? When the gun goes off, you take off like a Marine headed for the slopchute! You go to the front and stay there as long as you can! This race is going to be won by the guy with the most heart, not by strategy. Nobody's in better shape than you, and I'll put your guts and heart up there with anyone! I'll see you when you break the tape, and might even arrange for you and Garbetti to have a long weekend after you kick some ass!"

BANG! Jack took off with every ounce of energy he had, and in the first quarter mile he was out front by fifty yards! The other runners were grouped together, knowing that the idiot way in front would fold.

He heard Al yell, "Run you son of a bitch!"

For some strange reason he didn't get tired or even breathe hard. The weeks of running with a nine-pound M-1 rifle, cartridge belt with canteen, and a pack over his shoulders made the mile run seem like a stroll on the beach. The only challenge was for second

106

place, as Jack Harrington broke the tape at least thirty yards ahead of the number two runner.

Lt. Trimble's Dick Tracy jaw opened with a flashing smile as he pounded Jack on the back.

"Well, that takes care of the strategy theory! It shows what pumps through the heart of a true Marine!"

As amazing as Jack's feat was, Garbetti's may have been even more astounding. Lt. Trimble approached Al.

"Garbetti, you'll get three opportunities, and obviously your best effort will stand. The usual strategy for shot-putters is to save a little energy for shot numbers 2 and 3. Forget about that! Put every ounce of strength into the first shot! I want you to lead the pack after the first round! The others will wonder who the hell this guy is with the leading score, and start to press and throw off their timing. Do you understand me? Oh, by the way, I told Harrington that if you both won, I'd arrange for a long weekend for you. He's taken care of his half … now go out there and kick some ass!"

The sixteen-pound shot looked the size of a golf ball in Al's paw-like hand, and Al's first effort was as if he'd been a shot-putter all his life. No one came close to the Herculean heave, as the other competitors folded. At the awards ceremony, Major O'Donnell presented the first, second, and third place ribbons.

As he handed Jack his award, he said, in almost a whisper, "It's nice to see you doing something useful with your time, Private!"

There was a slight smile on the major's face as Jack answered.

"Thank you, Sir, for this and for past considerations!"

Chapter 24

The Sixth Naval Fleet continually cruised the Mediterranean in the early 1950's, and with them, at the ready, was always a battalion of F.M.F. Marines. The 1st Battalion, 6th Marines were scheduled for the six-month cruise, and would leave on September 2nd, 1951. Lt. Trimble was scheduled to be released from active duty in a month or two, so was transferred to other duties and wouldn't be on the training cruise.

He met with the S-2 section before the regiment packed their gear and headed for Morehead City to board ship.

"Being called back to active duty was a shock for me and my family. We had just moved into our first home, and my job was going well. But, as you all know by now, when the Commandant calls and your fellow Marines need you, you pack your trash and move out. People on the outside don't understand the full meaning of 'Semper Fidelis', but we know 'Always Faithful' means just that. We're always faithful to our fellow Marines! At the outset, I told you I would run your asses into the ground. Was I bullshitting you?"

"No, Sir!" they smiled in agreement.

"Well, I never succeeded because you always came back for more, and I'm extremely proud to have served with each and every one of you! If you serve in Korea, there will be no second chances when the shit hits the fan, so always remember the things you've learned so well. Your training, along with your stamina and heart, will bring you through.

"It's not bullshit when I tell you my thoughts and spirit will be with you along the way. Lt. Brookside will be your new S-2 officer, and I suppose I piled on the shit a little when I told him you're the best Marines in the regiment, but that's my true feeling. I wish you well for many years to come!"

Harrington and Garbetti never thought they'd actually miss the lieutenant if he left. However, as they headed for the slopchute that night they both knew that they would miss one of the great Marine officers, who had pushed them to altitudes they never dreamed of reaching. It was true. His spirit would remain with them forever. They polished off far too many beers ... most of them with a toast to Lieutenant Trimble!

Chapter 25

In 1944, Jack had taken the ferry from Boston to Provincetown. A friend's father ran the Sea Scout Camp in Wellfleet during the summer, and the kid had invited Jack to stay with him for a couple of weeks. The trip was unforgettable because he was so sick he wanted to die! He vowed he'd never get on any type of boat again, and here he was about to board the *U.S.S. Cambria, A.P.A. #36* in Morehead City, North Carolina.

Crossing the Atlantic had to be a hell of a lot rougher than a few miles to Provincetown, and living on board ship for six months had to be a bitch. Then he thought, *Stop your fucking complaining! You're getting **paid** to see Italy, Spain, Greece, and the French Riviera! It's a hell of a lot better than Huntington Prep or climbing around in an attic insulating!*

The *Cambria* was a troop ship that carried the entire 1st Battalion, so you can imagine the sleeping quarters for the troops.

The canvas cots were hung about six high on metal posts, and you had one hell of a climb if you were on top! There were only about 3 feet between cots, and Jack was above Al about 15 feet up from the deck. It was their new home away from home.

The ship left Morehead City and headed toward the first port of call, Oran, Algeria. It took all twelve days crossing the Atlantic for Jack to get his sea legs and get rid of that terrible motion sickness. Big Al had no problems. The rough seas didn't phase him at all.

One of the Navy corpsmen with us said, "Garbetti, you're the only fucking guy I ever saw who could eat a greasy pork chop in the middle of a fucking hurricane, go back for seconds, and then watch the rest of us puke our guts out from seasickness!"

Entering the Straits of Gibralter meant that Oran was close, and liberty wasn't far off. Everyone attended sessions on 'proper behavior' in a foreign country. A staff sergeant covered everything in easy to understand statements.

"We would ask you people to keep your pecker in your pants, but realize that's like asking a bear not to shit in the woods! We also know that most Marines think with their dick, not their brains, so just in case you don't intend to spend your time at the local museum, let me give you the facts of life!

"Cat houses are like horse shit in Oran ... they're everywhere! So, although you all think you're Don Juan, you won't have to fuck with the preliminaries. You can pay your money, and wham-bam-thank you, m'am, you're on to bigger and better things. However, after you pull out of your lovely new acquaintance, wash your joint with the magic ointment the corpsmen will issue you and move out!

"Do not! I say, **Do not!** travel the streets alone! Stick to drinking beer. Some of the local high test will knock the shit out of you! If you really drink the wrong shit, you can go blind! Don't fuck with veiled snatches! A jarhead on the last Med cruise had his dick cut off for fucking around with some Mata Hari type! Don't buy jewelry from some fucking street vendor. You can do better in the 5 & 10 in Morehead City when you return to the States.

"The beer is warm as piss, and the food is lousy. In fact, you're better off eating C-rations than Arab food, but right now I know food is the last thing on your mind. However, remember this: Marines always take care of each other in combat and on liberty, and you know what the old gunny always says: 'There's never been a bad piece of ass or blow job. Some are just better than others!' I can guarantee you pussy in Oran won't be the best you ever have, so make sure you don't get so fucked up that you can't look forward to entering the promised land at a later date!"

"I'm sure the company commander would have put it differently, but it would have taken hours, and the meaning wouldn't be as clear," laughed Jack.

Al agreed, and said, "Let's toss a coin to see who gets laid first!"

With three days in Oran, a third of the troops had liberty each day. Liberty call was at 1200 hours, and you'd better be walking back up the gangway by 2300 hours or you'd be in deep shit! Jack and Al got off the ship, settled in at a table outside a restaurant on the sidewalk, and ordered a beer. They had a couple of beers and then checked in on one of the whorehouses. Once in the sack, it took Jack all of about fifteen seconds to reach ecstasy, as they say. It took Al much longer ... about eighteen seconds! Then, it was off to some serious bar hopping, and maybe a little more ecstasy later on!

They left the watering hole at around 1800 hours, and it was dark outside. As they headed down the street a cab driver walked over and said, "Most beautiful woman in Algeria in my cab!"

Being three-quarters in the bag they said, "How much?"

They continued to walk, and when the driver said, "Ten dollars!" they laughed.

Al answered, "We don't want to fuck Marilyn Monroe! Are you crazy?"

"You look! You look!" He pulled them gently by the arm toward the cab.

114

The woman in the back seat was dressed in a long, white, flowing gown, and wore a see-through veil. You didn't have to be a beauty contest judge to know immediately that this passenger was a knockout!

"For Christ's sake, Jack! She's wearing a fucking veil!" whispered Al.

"Do you think this cab driver is going to fuck with a guy as big as you are? I'm not exactly a midget either!" whispered Jack. "We don't have ten bucks, but this is what I'll do." Jack took off the Tufts College ring with the crest set in a black stone that Chuck had given him.

"This ring is worth a fortune!" said Jack. "It's yours for the whole deal. We both get laid. You supply us with beer wherever you take us, and then drive us back to the ship!"

The cabbie looked at the ring carefully, and nodded to the half stiff Marines to get in the cab. They sat on each side of the girl as the cab headed out of downtown into the hilly streets surrounding Oran. Jack, with his arm around the girl, slowly did his imitation of Tyrone Power. He kissed her neck and face, felt the important parts of her upper body, and finally put his hand under the left side of her long, robe-like gown. He ran his hand slowly up her thigh in search of the promised land. As his hand was about to hit home base, he felt a huge hand in the strategic spot. It was

115

Big Al! Jack looked up, and there was Al grinning as he tried to hold back his laughter. Then, they both laughed hysterically!

In the room they were brought to, Jack said, "Al, it's only right that I go first. It was my ring! Besides, your dick is much bigger than mine. If I went second, she wouldn't even know I was in there!"

Al laughed. "O.K. Do you think I can finish half a beer before you're through?"

The ride back to the ship was filled with laughter when Jack said, "I always knew that college ring would lead to something great!"

Chapter 26

Fun and games were over as they cruised toward Sardinia and the first of seven mock landings over the next five months.

Climbing down thick rope nets from the *Cambria* into LCVP's to head toward the beach can be hairy, to say the least, especially when the sea is rough. The S-2 section hit the beach and moved inland for about six miles, where a bivouac area would be set. For the next three days they would participate in live fire infantry and artillery problems.

The sound of thousands of exploding rounds gave every Marine, who had yet to experience combat, a small taste of the sounds of death. There were even a few short rounds that landed far too close for comfort! The S-2 section realized real fast what Lt. Trimble had drilled into them: "No matter where you are, always be a step ahead and pick out a hollow spot in the terrain to head for when incoming hits. It could well save your life!"

The second night, while in the shelter half that they shared, Al said to Jack, "You know we're fucking crazy! We've always been told never to volunteer, and we've already officially volunteered to go to Korea. Let's not send another request through channels, at least until we get back to Lejeune!"

"I'm with you, Al! I didn't like the sound of that heavy shit either!" Jack said seriously.

The fleet headed toward Naples, their main port. They would return on four other occasions in between landings around the Mediterranean. Naples was a great city, and Al, being as Italian as they come, couldn't wait to get there.

"We'll be shacking up with real women now, and eating the best food in the world!" Al said at least every hour on the hour.

They went through almost the same liberty speech from the S/Sgt., but he had something to add. He showed them a poster-sized picture of Lucky Luciano, a gangster from Chicago, who had been involved with Murder Incorporated and deported back to Italy for life. They were told that under no circumstances were they to associate with him or anyone with him. They really didn't understand why, but didn't care either, as they were sure he wouldn't want anything to do with a shipload of Marines anyway.

The Minoosian brothers, both Navy corpsmen with the 6th Marines, came back from liberty the first night. They told Jack and

Al to head toward the 'Snake Pit', a bar/restaurant with great food, women, and rooms upstairs! Naturally, that's where they headed the next night on the first of many in Naples during the next five months.

They ordered a beer at their small table and in about ten minutes the waiter appeared with two more beers.

He said, "Compliments of Mr. Luciano", as he pointed over to a dark corner of the restaurant.

"Jesus Christ! We can't drink this beer can we?" Al said nervously.

Jack thought back to what Bob Langer had once said when free beers were sent over to him. '*Never look a gift horse in the fucking mouth, and besides, you insult someone when you refuse their hospitality. Just pick up the beer, look over at their table, and give a little toast!*'

"Al, just do what I do!"

They both toasted the dark corner table with their new bottles of beer.

In a few minutes a guy appeared at their table. He was dressed in a suit and tie like the other three with Mr. Luciano.

He said, "Mr. Luciano would like to see you", and invited them to the corner table. There a charming man with a very low voice asked us a number of questions about the United States, where we were from, and how long we'd be away from home.

Dinner, drinks, and interesting conversation were all courtesy of Mr. Luciano.

As he left with his entourage, he told Jack and Al to stay as his guests as long as they wanted to. An hour later a well-dressed man suggested that, if they wished, rooms were available upstairs, compliments of Mr. Luciano.

As they headed up the stairs, Al said, "This must be a fucking dream!"

Jack answered, "Somebody has to do it! It might as well be us!"

They headed back to the *Cambria,* vowing to never mention the Luciano story. They would frequent the 'Snake Pit' many more times, but never did see Mr. Luciano again. However, they did see the ladies of the evening they had met, and being personal friends of Mr. Lucky Luciano certainly didn't hurt their reputation as men of the world!

Before going to Augusta Bay, Sicily for more landings, the *Cambria* docked at Valletta, Malta. Malta is a speck of Mediterranean rock rising out of the sea, and was the most bombed spot on earth during World War II. Al and Jack were happy to go ashore and pull liberty in a mountainless, English-speaking country. Every building built there was made of local soap/sandstone, so the city was a huge fortress. The beer was warm and rich, the food good, and the people extremely friendly.

Everyone regretted shipping out and getting ready to climb down the landing nets again!

Chapter 27

The weeks flew by! Back to Naples - - Golfe Juan, France - - Malta again - - A landing at Suda Bay, Crete - - Naples again. Then, the biggest operation of the cruise - - Phaleron Bay, Greece.

At their morning formation on board ship, Lt. Brookside announced that the upcoming operation was an extremely important one. Two men from S-2 would join a dozen Navy frogmen on board the submarine *U.S.S. Tigrone*. The frogmen would leave the submarine in a large rubber boat, and place explosives near the shore that would be discharged before the landing craft hit the beach to simulate an actual live-fire landing.

Two S-2 Marines would leave in a two-man boat, and set up a communication center on an island a quarter-mile off the beach. They would stay the night, and call in air support as forward observers for the Marine air wing that was on a carrier at sea.

Lt. Brookside announced that Harrington, being the strongest swimmer in the section, would go, and then asked who, if anybody, had experience with boats and outboard motors. Garbetti immediately spoke up.

"Sir, being from the Boston area, I spent a lot of time during the summer around boats, and my family owned a small boat with an outboard motor."

This, of course, was all bullshit, but Lt. Brookside immediately picked Garbetti as the second man.

Harrington and Garbetti were transferred by breeches buoy, along with the lieutenant, to the destroyer escort, *U.S.S. Cobb.* They then headed for a rendezvous with the submarine. The weather turned so bad that they actually had to be strapped into their bunk if they tried to sleep. Once again, Garbetti was the only one that didn't even get queasy. They were able to transfer over to the sub, and it was a whole new experience to spend time under water to avoid the awful weather.

They were briefed continually by the lieutenant, who would be brought into the beach on the morning of the landing as an observer. The calm after the storm was a blessing. They prepared their gear on the submarine deck as Brookside, along with the captain and executive officer of the submarine, watched from the conning tower.

The frogmen left in a huge boat loaded down with their gear, and then the Marines loaded up the small two-man boat with their gear. A couple of sailors helped get the boat into the water. Jack and Al got in and pushed off from the sub. Garbetti was in the stern of the raft, where a small horsepower outboard hooked into a large rubber flange that hung into the ocean.

As the observers watched from the conning tower, Garbetti pulled the starter cord two or three times with no results. He then rose up on one knee to put more strength into pulling the cord. He pulled so hard that the small motor slipped out of the rubber flange, flew six feet in the air over Jack's head and the bow of the boat … and into the ocean!

Jack flashed a glance toward the conning tower and saw a shocked Lt. Brookside, but was sure he saw a smile cross the faces of the Navy officers. Without skipping a beat Jack turned, put the standby oars into the permanent oarlocks, and started rowing toward the island.

As they moved away from the sub, he said, "I'm sure glad you had all that experience with those fucking outboard motors, Al!"

Their laughter couldn't be heard from the submarine, but it lasted for at least ten pulls on the oars. They pulled the boat up on a small beach area, and camouflaged it with sand and rocks for the night.

It was a hell of a climb with a full pack, radio, and weapon to get up the hill to the high point of the island. They set up their shelter half, checked in on the radio, and prepared to get some sleep, with each man taking a shift of staying awake. At sunrise, they'd do their job and then join the forces on the beach.

Jack awoke to strange noises, which were getting louder and louder. He looked out from the small tent, and they were surrounded by hundreds of goats!

He screamed, "For Christ's sake, Al! There are fucking goats everywhere!"

They yelled at the goats and stomped on the ground, which sent them running away. The sun was coming up, and the roar of planes came overhead as Marine Corsairs flew low over the island. In a matter of seconds, the planes had flown over the landing area before the Marine assault began.

Jack and Al had really fucked up this time. Falling asleep on watch was a court martial offense, and who knows what the penalty for fucking up air support for a landing was! With fear in their eyes, and that sick feeling you get when you know you're in deep shit, they packed up all the gear into the boat and rowed to the main landing area. By the time they arrived, the operation was well underway. They were told the command post was about a mile inland on the high ground.

They double-timed to the C.P., and as they approached they saw Lt. Brooksde and other battalion officers. Sure they were going to face numerous charges, they came to attention in front of the lieutenant and saluted.

He saluted back, and said, "You men did the finest job we've ever seen of co-ordinating the air support! Good work!"

They were told to join up with the rest of the section further up the road. Lt. Brookside had never heard a more enthusiastic reply.

"Thank you, Sir!"

Two very relieved Marines headed up the road!

Chapter 28

The Med cruise wasn't all amphibious landings, drinking beer, and getting laid. From their homeport, Naples, they traveled to Rome. St. Peter's was magnificent with it's colonnade surrounded square. The catacombs, Vatican City, and the Sistine Chapel, as Al said, were a hell of a lot more impressive than Scolley Square in Boston.

"Yeah," agreed Jack, "but, I don't see 'Peaches, Queen of Shake' hanging around here!"

Pompeii, Capri, Malta, Cannes, and Nice, France were great. In France, Jack and Al stocked up on Chanel, Arpege, and Joy perfume for their family and female friends in the States. Athens, Greece was fascinating, but on one visit the local watering hole favorite, Ouzo, got the best of both Al and Jack. A hangover from drinking Ouzo is like no other!

On the last day of January 1951, the *Cambria* pulled up anchor and headed through the straits for the States. Fourteen days later they docked in Morehead City, and headed back to Camp Lejeune. Jack and Al arranged for a ten-day leave, and also decided to provide their own transportation for the run to Boston. They bought a 1949 Chrysler, and paid for it by transporting Marines to New York City on the weekends.

Al had all kinds of relatives in Tuckahoe and Mamaroneck, not far from the City. They'd take turns every other weekend taking riders to the City, spend Saturday and Saturday night at Aunt Anna's, then pick up the riders at a bar next to Penn Station around noon on Sunday and head back to Lejeune! Jack and Al always said it was amazing how far a guy would drive in hopes of hitting the promised land!

At 1700 hours on a Friday, the Chrysler would pull into the bus station on the base. Hundreds of Marines would be leaving for the weekend.

"Twenty bucks round trip to New York!" either Jack or Al would yell out the window.

In seconds, they'd have five passengers and head toward the gate to begin the 'Indianapolis 600'! The road from J'ville to Kinston to Wilson and Rt. 301 was 70 miles or so, and it was packed with Marines jockeying for position!

Local and state police were at the ready every Friday and late Sunday night to nail as many Marines as possible for imitating the famous race drivers of the day. They only stopped for gas, would hit Penn Station around 0400 hours, and get back before 0600 Monday morning. Jack and Al always made incredible time on their New York run, so built up a following of customers and never had to worry about filling the car.

A member of the S-2 section from China Grove, North Carolina, had just purchased a 1950 Ford. To help with the car payments, he asked Jack to take a load of Marines to New York for him.

"This will be great, Al. We can follow each other to the City, and then go to Tuckahoe for the weekend … or leave one car in Tuckahoe and go to Boston."

After dropping off the riders in the city, they headed for the West Side Highway and raced toward Westchester County. The 10-cent toll takers near the George Washington Bridge must have been scared shitless when a Chrysler and a Ford drove through the tolls neck and neck at over sixty miles per hour!

Al's many relatives treated Jack like a member of the family. The Italian meals that Aunt Anna would cook put anything they had eaten in Italy to shame! They had wonderful times in Tuckahoe, and Jack dated Al's cousin, Fiona.

"I know you like a fucking book, Harrington! For some reason girls always like you, but you're the most fickle son of a bitch around! Remember, we're not back at the Snake Pit, so don't fuck around with my cousin unless you're serious!" Al warned him.

Chapter 29

Marine Corps promotions didn't come easily, so moving from private first class to corporal was a big deal. The S-2 section lined up to 'pin' the corporal stripes on Jack and Al. Each member took great pleasure in 'punching' on the stripes on each upper arm. A full-swing punch from ten guys makes your arms look like you'd painted them with black and blue paint, but it's a ritual that goes with the territory.

However, the free beers at the slopchute took away some of the pain. Besides, maybe the Marine Corps needed N.C.O.'s in Korea more than privates, so Jack and Al continued to send in requests for duty in Korea.

Jack knew what Bob Langer would say: "You asshole! I told you to never volunteer! When some fucking gook is zeroing in on you, you'll wish you had minded your own fucking business!"

133

The next few months were filled with continuous training, and trips to New York and Boston. Jack and Al worked a few days liberty pass, and went to Tuckahoe for one night and then on to Boston. Before leaving for Boston, they stopped to have a pizza and beer in a local restaurant. As Jack went from the restaurant side through the bar to the men's room, he noticed a complete tap beer cooling system sitting on the end of the bar. It was a big, metal cooler box with copper coils inside, which you covered with ice. The beer went through the freezing coils from the beer keg through a hose to the beer tap, and was then served ice cold.

Jack reported the find to Al, and they both agreed it would be perfect in the bar in the basement of his house in Newton.

"The cooler is sitting at the end of the bar, right near the door that goes out to the parking lot. First, open the trunk of the car in the parking lot, then come in and watch me at the other end of the bar. I'll order a beer and keep the bartender busy with some line of bullshit. You take the cooler box out to the car, and put the hose and beer tap near the door. I'll get it on my way out."

Jack sat talking to the bartender, and saw Al make his move. Saying, "Take care" to the bartender, he headed out the back, picking up the prize on the way out. They drove toward the Merritt Parkway, and in years to come had many ice-cold brews that ran through those wonderful copper coils from New York!

When they returned to the base, Jack was given orders to move out to the rifle range for two weeks of qualification for the Camp Lejeune rifle team. Shooters with scores over 225 were recruited for competition to determine who would be assigned to duty with the team that would represent Camp Lejeune in marksmanship events around the country. Officers and enlisted men alike were involved in the competition.

For two days in a row Jack was next to a salty major on the firing line from the 600-yard range. Regular qualification in the Marine Corps for long-range shooting was from 500 yards, but the distance was increased for the national shooting matches. The major continually pumped shots into the 20-inch black bull's eye. Jack had a few shots in the black, but nowhere near the major's number.

During a brief break the major said, "Marine, your right elbow is set about a quarter of an inch too far away from your body. Pull it in a hair and you'll be steadier and in the black".

The slight adjustment did the trick, and Jack thanked the major.

"You're a hell of a marksman, Marine. Someday you may get the opportunity to fire the old 'Springfield 03' and then you'll be in the black on every shot!"

Just as Jack was thinking he might have a chance to make the rifle team, he was called back to mainside for further orders.

The sergeant major had received the orders that he and Al had been pushing for. He was going to Korea!

"Garbetti's orders must be here too, Top. We've been sending our requests at the same time."

"Harrington, do you think Headquarters Marine Corps sits around on their ass at Eighth & I Streets in D.C. and says, 'Oh, wait a fucking minute! We'd better send Garbetti with Harrington so they can play grab ass together over in Gooneyland'? You both rolled the dice, and it depends on how you look at it as to who the fucking winner is! I'll have your thirty-day leave papers drawn up, and you'll be ready to saddle up in a day or two. I've heard about your speed runs to the fucking north. I might even arrange for Garbetti to get a long weekend to ride shotgun with you!"

The Top looked at Harrington eyeball-to-eyeball and said, "Semper Fi, Harrington! The Marine Corps is in good shape with men like you and Garbetti! Good luck to you!"

"I know it's fucked up, Al" said Jack, "but, it has to have something to do with the time we have left to serve. I joined about three months before you did, and the tour of duty in Korea is one year. My fucking time is running out. You'll probably get orders to go in a month or two. I'll pull my thirty-day leave, and head for Camp Pendleton on the coast. Who knows … we could still go over at the same time. Now, let's hit the gate and head north!"

Chapter 30

They stopped in Tuckahoe, and Jack said goodbye to all the relatives who had been so wonderful to him. He promised to write Fiona, and then they took off for Boston.

After being home for a few days, Jack's father asked if he'd like to work a couple of days with Bob Langer and his crew. Jack jumped at the chance.

Bob greeted him with, "Your old man told me you were heading over close to the 'Land of the Rising Sun'. You know there's a town on the fucking north shore named after you. It's 'Marblehead'! You volunteered didn't you? Don't even answer because I know you did! You want to find out for yourself what it's all about … any true jarhead does! It ain't no picnic in the fucking park, believe me, but for some strange reason, I wish I was going with you!"

Over a number of beers after work, Langer said, "Jackie Boy, your hitch in the Marine Corps is something you'll always be proud of, and I'm proud of you, too. I knew fucking 'A' you'd volunteer for the real thing, and when you come back I'll personally take you to Jack's Lighthouse and dinner at Durgin & Park! Keep your head down!"

Many of Jack's close friends got together for one hell of a party before he left for the coast. Don Dunlop was on leave from the Navy, and Bobby Gregg and Bob Kell came home from college. Jim came home from General Motors Institute in Flint, Michigan, Dave Connors from the Air Force, and Dick Foran from Nichols Junior College, just to name a few.

They headed to Marconi's in Framingham, which was known to serve a pitcher of beer to anyone who could say 'pizza'. When that closed for the night, they went to close The Last Chance just over the Newton line in Watertown.

The Chance served musky beer that ran through a draft beer system that hadn't been cleaned since Ted Williams hit the blooper ball into the bullpen at Fenway in the 1946 All Star game! The older, grizzled waitress, Mabel, loved hearing, "Mabel! Mabel! Another round of Black Label!" The Carling brewery was out in Natick, and people swore they used unfiltered water from Lake Cochituate to brew Carling Black Label beer! But, at the hours 2300 to 0100, all beer tastes good, and Mabel looked like Rita Hayworth!

The next day Jack called the Anderson's to see how Carol was doing, and to get her phone number in California. Much to his surprise, he found out that Carol was in New York City for a semester of joint studies with Columbia students. He couldn't dial her number fast enough, and her reaction was the same as his.

"You've got to come down for a weekend, Jack. Please! You can't go to Korea without seeing me!"

Whoever answered the phone at 'The Little Italy' restaurant in Brooklyn wasn't interested in conversation.

"What's your business with Carmen?"

"He's a friend of mine from our Marine Corps days at Parris Island. I'm going to be in New York, and I was hoping he might be around."

"Give me a phone number where he can reach ya. I'll call him right now."

It was obvious that Carmen was glad to hear from Jack.

"Have you made fucking general yet? How the hell are ya? You're coming to New York? Where are ya staying?"

Jack hadn't given much thought to that. He told Carmen he'd try and get a cheap hotel room somewhere, and hoped he could see him.

"You're coming down on Friday? O.K. You're coming by train? Grab a cab from Grand Central and go to *The Plaza Hotel.* It's on Central Park West and Fifth Avenue with a nice view of Central Park. There'll be a room reserved for you there. You and your girlfriend have dinner with me Friday night. I'll call ya at the hotel."

The cab dropped Jack off at *The Plaza*, and he was shocked when he saw the hotel. Talk about *The Ritz* in Boston! This place would cost three times as much. He went to the front desk to inquire about the price.

"Mr. Harrington, your accommodations have been taken care of by Mr. Manero, along with any services you may require while at our establishment. It's a pleasure to welcome you to *The Plaza.*"

It wasn't a room. It was a suite overlooking Central Park. Two bottles of iced champagne, fruit, and several different choices of cheese and crackers sat on the table, along with bottles of iced beer. As Jack cracked open a bottle of beer, the phone rang.

"The flunky at the front desk tells me you checked in. I'll be down in two minutes!" yelled Carmen. As Carmen bear-hugged Jack, he spoke through his laughter. "Beats the shit out of those fucking huts at P.I., huh? How the hell are ya?"

"I'm great, Carmen, but I haven't got a pot to piss in. I can't stay here!"

"Don't be an oongatz! You think I'd send you here if you had to pay these fucking people? One of our business associates is the president of the union for all the hotel workers in New York. So, the rooms you have, and I have above you, are just in appreciation for what a good job the hotel workers do for all the guests. You don't have to know any details, Jack, but just understand that you never open your wallet while you're at *The Plaza* or with me. Capeece?

"Yeah, I'm out of the Corps," Carmen said. "They sent me to Motor Transport School, and then to Quantico to play chauffeur to a bunch of fucking officers. My family made arrangements for me to get my discharge a little early, so I'm back in civilian life. You told me you're going to Korea. Are you sure you want to go? Because if you don't, I can arrange for you to not go, ya know what I mean? O.K., O.K. You're a dumb shit, and you want to go, but think about it.

"My girlfriend and I want to take you and ... what's her name?... Carol to dinner. We'll go downtown to the best Italian place you've ever been to. Is that O.K. with you? We'll meet you in the lobby at seven o'clock."

At four-thirty Jack met Carol in the lobby of *The Plaza*. She no longer had that high-school kid look. She was a knockout, and as she entered the hotel heads turned in her direction.

"Jack," she whispered as he hugged her. "You look like the Marine on those recruiting posters. I'm sure glad to see you!"

A bellhop appeared out of nowhere.

"Mr. Harrington, please let me take that bag."

He took Carol's overnight bag toward the elevator. At the door to the suite, Jack reached for a tip.

"Oh, no, sir. Mr. Manero has taken care of everything."

Chapter 31

As Jack opened the champagne, Carol was looking out at Central Park.

Turning to him in utter amazement, she laughingly said, "How the hell did you ever arrange all this, and how will we ever pay for it?"

He briefly explained their good fortune, but he was so anxious to kiss Carol over and over again that they just forgot about the details.

"Come on into the bedroom. I want to show you something," Jack said.

"Ill bet you do!" smiled Carol.

On the huge bed were two beautiful white bathrobes. Quick as a flash, Carol was naked and pulling on her robe, as Jack did the same.

She turned on the shower in the huge master bath and said, "Let's not waste water. We'll shower together."

Only half dried off, they rolled under the blankets and wanted the weekend to never end!

After meeting Carmen and his girlfriend, Cindy, in the lobby, they approached a long, black limousine parked in front of *The Plaza.* Jack remembered the driver from La Guardia airport when he and Carmen arrived after boot camp. He still looked like Ted Liberty, but come to find out, his name was Bruno and he was always at Carmen's side.

"We'll go to The Sicilian, Bruno, and show our guests what real Italian food is!"

Carmen looked at Carol and told her what a great pleasure it was for Cindy and him to meet her, and to call him if there was ever anything she needed when she was in New York.

No menus were brought to their table. Carmen ordered for everyone, and course after course of the greatest Italian food they had ever eaten kept appearing at the table, along with delicious wine. Carmen, of course, asked Jack about what he had done for the past year and a half in the Marine Corps. When Jack told him about the Mediterranean cruise and the meeting with Lucky Luciano, Carmen was amazed.

"Luciano is a close friend of our family's, Jack, and my father will get a hell of a kick out of your seeing him in Naples."

He beckoned an older man over to the table, and introduced Mr. Cattanaci to Carol, Jack, and Cindy.

"Jack met Lucky Luciano in Naples a few months ago, Cat."

Well, you'd think Jack was a long-lost friend of Mr. Cattanaci. They talked for at least fifteen minutes. When he was leaving, he offered Jack carte blanche at the restaurant whenever he was in New York!

"The big Cat is a good man to know, Jack. There is nothing, and I mean <u>nothing</u>, that he can't take care of!"

Carmen motioned Jack toward the men's room before they left The Sicilian. He handed Jack an elastic-bound packet of crisp new bills.

"I want you to have plenty of cash while you're here, and in California before you go to Korea. You may want to leave Carol some spending money, too. Remember the time in the train at Yemassee when you told me you would have pissed your pants if you were me, and then you told my family at the airport how no one fucked with me at Parris Island? That meant a lot to me, Jack, and I'll never forget it. This is a gift from me to you, and you can always count on me if you need anything.

"We'll drive you and Carol back to *The Plaza*. We can't join you tomorrow night, but arrangements are made for you to go to The Rainbow Room. It's up in Rockefeller Plaza and the view of the city is beautiful. Bruno will pick you up at eight o'clock, and bring you back whenever you want. Don't even think about taking your wallet out of your pocket!"

They said their goodbyes outside *The Plaza*.

"Carmen, how the hell can I ever pay you back for all this?"

"My payback, my friend, will be when you return safely from Korea, and come to see me again in the City. Semper Fi, and take care of yourself!"

Chapter 32

The long weekend in New York was like a fairy tale, a dream come true, but there was also a terrible sadness that being together, at least for a while, was over. Jack put five hundred dollars in an envelope along with a note, and slipped it into Carol's overnight bag.

Dear Carol,

Please keep half of this for when we're together again. Please buy something for yourself that will remind you of me with the other half. I'll take care of myself because I have to see you again ...and you do the same.

I love you!

Jack

Sitting in the club car on the way back to Boston was the only way to go. A few cold beers and lunch made the time fly by. Smiling to himself, Jack thought of his total pay for the year

1951 in the Marine Corps – a shade over one thousand dollars. The money packet that Carmen Manero had handed to Jack held two one-hundred dollar bills, ten fifty-dollar bills, twenty twenty-dollar bills, and a few tens and fives mixed in for good measure. He ordered another beer, and wondered about just how Carmen made his living. Jack determined real fast that he would leave well enough alone.

Saying goodbye to your family for a long period of time is always difficult, but it was more so for Jack's family members because they knew that the final destination involved a war that no one completely understood. The only thing Jack's mother, father, and sisters, Ann and Julie, knew was that there were a lot of Marines being killed in a country called Korea.

The flight to Los Angeles was one of mixed emotions for Jack. When he landed in L.A., he called home, as promised, to report a safe trip … and his spirits flew! Al Garbetti had called. He had just received orders to go to Korea, and after a thirty-day leave he would be at Camp Pendleton!

That night Jack dropped a note to Carmen Manero in care of The Little Italy restaurant.

Carmen,

It was great to see you again. Carol and I had a perfect weekend, and we have you to thank for that. You were much too generous in every way, Carmen, and I'll never forget it. I'll call you when I return to California from the vacation in Korea. After all, it can't be as bad as Parris Island, can it?

Say 'Hello' to Cindy and your family. Oh, and ask Bruno if he'd mind driving me from California to Brooklyn in about a year!

Thanks again. Semper Fi!

Jack

Chapter 33

For some strange reason Jack had had visions of arriving in California, getting on a troop ship, and heading for Korea. Well, it didn't work out that way! There was an area at Pendleton, called 'the staging area', where all personnel going to Korea on the next draft were housed. Each month a new draft of Marines left for Korea.

Jack was scheduled for the 28th draft, which would leave before Christmas. Before debarking, everyone had to go through cold weather training at Pickle Meadows in the Sierra Nevada Mountains, and then more night time infantry training. This meant that Jack would be in the staging area for a while.

In the slopchute that night, one of the guys at the table was from Massachusetts, not far from Newton. Ron Torrance had been stationed at Pendleton for the past year or so, and was a truck driver in motor transport. Ronnie said he knew all the good joints in L.A. and Hollywood, and asked Jack to spend liberty over the weekend in town with a couple of other guys who had a car.

Ron Torrance was a Jimmy Cagney lookalike, but much bigger. They showered before heading to L.A., and it was easy to see that Ron could be a walking advertisement for Ted Liberty's Scolley Square artwork. On the cheeks of his ass were boat propellers, "Twin screws like Errol Flynn's yacht," bragged Ron. Under each nipple on his chest was blazoned 'Sweet' on the right, and 'Sour' on the left. His thigh was adorned with a large, red cherry with the caption, 'Here's mine. Where's yours?' The fingers of his hands spelled out 'GOOD LUCK', and unlocked handcuffs around each wrist were set off by a bluebird stating, 'Free as a bird.' There was an array of snakes, spiders, and, of course, the Marine Corps bulldog in a place of honor on his right arm.

When Ron went to the head, a kid from the motor pool announced to no one in particular, "Don't ever fuck with Ron. He'd take Rocky Marciano down in a flash, and then beat the shit out of his corner man just for the hell of it. He don't play by the Marquis of Queensbury rules. He plays by Ronnie Torrance rules: Kick 'em, punch 'em, and never give a sucker an even break!"

They arrived in Hollywood, and the two other guys went their own way. Jack followed Ronnie into a bar that was packed with people, half of them Marines.

They ordered a beer, and the bartender said, "Ron, you know I can't serve you in here!"

"C'mon! C'mon! I'm going to Korea in a few weeks. I won't cause any fucking trouble," smiled Ronnie.

"I can't, Ron. I'll lose my job if the boss comes in!"

"Fuck you and the horse you rode in on! Come on, Jack. We've been thrown out of better places!"

The next watering hole was the same story, and at the third one the bartender gave the same spiel. Ronnie went through his 'going to Korea' routine, and the bartender said, "O.K.! O.K.! But, I'm telling ya, Ron, no fights!"

At around 2400 hours, and feeling no pain, Ron suggested they get some sack time. To Jack's amazement, they headed into the lobby of the Beverly Hills Hotel, where a room cost more than they made in about three months! They walked through the lobby and down two flights of stairs to the basement area, where a guy yelled, "Hey, Ron, how ya doing?"

In a large storeroom were a couple of dozen single portable beds all made up with clean sheets in case someone needed an extra bed in their room.

"I'll have to wake you up a little before 6:30 as usual, Ron, before the day shift comes on."

At the wake up call, Ronnie said, "Thanks, Charlie. We'll probably see ya at Charlene's tonight."

153

Ronnie was a good guy to know, even though some of the high-class Hollywood establishments didn't care for his business. Charlene and two other girls rented a small house. Ronnie said every weekend was party time, and he was right. Practically everyone who came and went knew Ron, and Jack couldn't wait to include Al Garbetti in the Hollywood scene!

Jack found out the next morning why Ron had been 'deep-sixed' from a few establishments. They had walked to a diner-type restaurant that had small outside tables almost on the sidewalk. Jack and Ron ordered large orange juice and a couple of doughnuts each. They were in civilian clothes, but had on Marine Corps shoes so most people could immediately tell that they were from Pendleton.

One fairly tough-looking guy at a nearby table of three people said, "Coffee too strong for jarheads?" All three laughed.

Like a flash, Ronnie was at their table, and said, "Anything bothering you, fuckface?" as he looked at the guy who made the coffee remark.

As the guy stood up, Ron kicked him in the shin with all his might. The guy screamed and crumpled to the ground. Another guy, halfway out of his chair, was smashed in the face full-force with a right like Rocky Marciano's. The third guy hauled ass! Ron dragged the first guy to the curb, pushed his face between a car tire and the curb, and stomped on him once. A th-wump sound had to mean a mouthful of missing teeth. This all took place in about thirty seconds.

Ronnie said, "We'd better have breakfast somewhere else!"

No wonder his options were limited!

Later that day, Charlene made a definite pass at Jack. He put two and two together real fast and came up with Charlene and Jack equals a problem with Ronnie, which was an extremely bad idea! However, Jack did hit Ron with the question of whether or not Charlene was his girlfriend. Ron wasn't one to beat around the bush or mince words.

"In a few weeks we'll be freezing our asses off in Korea. You're a groundpounder, so you might just get your ass shot off. Any fucking moron can see she's got the hots for you, so you better make hay while the fucking sun still shines!"

That was good enough for Jack!

Chapter 34

Back at Pendleton they continued to run around the boondocks during the day, and hit the slopshute or Oceanside at night. In the slopshute, Ronnie ran into a guy he knew well, who was leaving in two days for Korea.

"Ron, give me fifty bucks, and you can have the Zephyr. The plates don't run out for a few months, so just drive the fucking thing into the ground or get your fifty bucks back from someone else. The only problem with it is when you push the clutch in to shift, you have to pull the rope I attached to it to get the clutch back out. It's easy to do, though. If you don't have the cash, I'll give you my mother's address, and you can send a money order to her."

Done! They now had a 1939 Lincoln Zephyr, and would collect five or ten bucks apiece from a few guys to pay for it. Jack dropped Al a note at his house, and told him he had a Lincoln waiting to transport him to Hollywood. He didn't bother to include that it was a 1939 shitbox with a rope-operated clutch!

Big Al was now **truly** Big Al! With his mother filling him with Italian chow for a month, he had packed on over twenty-five pounds, but, as he said, "I'll lose it during the next couple of weeks of running around these fucking California mountains!"

Pickle Meadows was a ball buster! It's in the Sierra Nevada Mountains, not far from Lake Tahoe and Reno, Nevada. It was in the Sonora Pass area, over 10,000 feet high, that many settlers in the 1800's froze to death making the trip through the rugged mountains there.

Everyone packed all their cold weather gear. After what seemed like a never-ending bus ride, they arrived at the base of the mountains. They headed up the trail toward more than five feet of snow and sub-zero weather. The group included many Marines who were office pinkies, truck drivers, cooks, or had other duties that had kept them from doing much physical exercise.

Halfway up the mountain with a full pack and weapons, both Jack and Al thought of Lt. Trimble. They weren't even breathing hard. Most of the long column of Marines were huffing and puffing like the wolf blowing those three fucking pigs out of their house!

Once again Garbetti and Harrington set up a shelter half, with Ronnie and another motor transport guy nearby. It was so cold that every few hours they were given fifteen or twenty minutes in warming huts in order to survive. They ran patrols every night with 'aggressors' on snowshoes and skis firing blanks, blowing horns, and yelling 'Die Marines!'

When they finally crawled into their sleeping bags, the 'aggressors' would attack again, knocking shelter halves down and demanding that all Marines surrender. Ronnie lunged at one 'aggressor', but slipped in the snow before nailing him. Good thing because he probably would have broken the guy's neck, and ended up in the Portsmouth Naval prison!

Back to Pendleton, and the realization that it was close to shipping out time. They would never be any colder than they were at Pickle Meadows, but damn near it in the hills of Korea! However, there would be many times they would yearn for aggressors firing blanks, instead of Chinese firing the real thing!

Chapter 35

The last long weekend could well have ended in disaster, but somehow the old Lincoln got them back to the base. There were a number of stories to embellish on during the fifteen days or so it would take to cross the Pacific!

First stop on Thursday night was Jack Teagarden's great bar. You never knew what well-known musicians might join the great trombone player in late night jazz sessions. The best way to begin what they hoped would be the weekend to end all weekends was to each drink two 'zombies', which would pave the way for a three day glow. Most bartenders would only serve you two zombies because each one had about five kinds of rum in it, and was like Lauren Bacall … tall and lethal!

After making the usual rounds, Ronnie told Al we all might as well check into the Beverly Hills Hotel early.

Al was shocked. "Are you fucking nuts? It'll cost us a fortune!"

Ron explained that he had celebrity status, and was welcome anytime … on the house! They checked into their basement suite, and the guy on duty greeted them.

"Hey, Ron! Hey, Jack! Long time no see!"

With everything set, it was decided to have one more beer at the first floor lounge.

"Ronnie," chimed in Charlie, "Walter's on the bar tonight. Just tell him you saw me, and he'll set you up … on the house!"

"Any friend of Charlie's is a friend of mine!" said Walter.

Ice cold beers hit the bar. Halfway through the first beer, a big, John Wayne lookalike stood behind them and ordered a beer. As he reached between Ron and Jack to get the beer, he bumped Ron's shoulder.

"Hey, give me a little room, will ya?" the guy asked.

Ron turned, looked at the guy, and said, "There's plenty of room at the other end of the bar, fuckface. Try your luck down there next time!"

"Who the hell do you think you're talking to? You fucking Marines are all alike … loud mouths!"

Jack asked Ron to take it easy, and was assured that it was okay.

Ron very quietly said, "Would you like to see just how loud my fucking mouth is out in the parking lot?"

He stood and looked up at the guy, who may have thought he really was John Wayne!

Ron walked slowly out the door, followed by the big guy. Ron's strategy in any kind of fight was to always get in the first blow, and never fight like a gentleman. As they reached the lot, Ronnie turned and kicked the guy in the balls. He screamed and clutched his family jewels. Ron grabbed him by the shirt and sport coat, pushed him up against a car, and gave him a shot to the jaw that ended the screams immediately. The knocked-out civilian slid to the sitting position and slumped against the car, as Ron walked back into the lounge.

"I think we'd better go down to our room before our new-found friend wakes up!" smiled Ron.

The next couple of days were spent making the rounds in L.A. and Hollywood, with one final get together at Charlene's. Before heading back to Pendleton, an 0200 breakfast was in order at the diner. They were laughing about the weekend events, but weren't causing any problems, when a lieutenant colonel in the Air Force approached the table.

"Will you Marines keep it down? This isn't a bar room!"

Ron was going to say something, but all three of them decided to just say, "Yes, Sir!"

The colonel went back to his booth and smiled at his woman companion.

"He's trying to impress that bitch with his fucking authority!" Al said, as they were about to leave. The check was paid and they were finishing their coffee, laughing about selling the Lincoln to someone else.

The colonel appeared again.

"How many times do you men have to be told to zip it up?"

"We're leaving right now, Sir", Jack said.

As they were getting up, the waitress brought the colonel a very full plate of pancakes and bacon. He poured syrup all over his meal, and Ron couldn't resist. He calmly walked over to the colonel's table.

"Excuse me, Sir!"

Ron picked up the plate and pushed it into the shocked colonel's chest. Syrup, butter, pancakes, and bacon dripped down his chest, covering his ribbons.

Ronnie said quietly, "Sir, if I were you I wouldn't move from that booth because I'll break your fucking neck!"

The stunned fly boy officer tried to clean up the mess, as the Marines made a rapid exit to the Lincoln.

Back at the base, they offered the same deal for the 1939 Zephyr to another jarhead ... fifty bucks. The registration still hadn't run out, the rope working the clutch still operated, and the car sure knew the way to Hollywood!

"We sent a $50 money order to our friend's mother. You can do the same thing for us, if you want," said Ron, and another Marine took charge of the wonderful old car!

Chapter 36

On a beautiful San Diego day, the troops waited on the dock to board ship for the long haul to Korea. The feelings that ran through Jack's mind were more in keeping with a cold, dismal, winter day in Boston. It was one thing to volunteer over and over to enter the war, but now it was put your money where your mouth is time. There was no turning back now.

Many of the hundreds of troops boarding ship on the sunlit day in California would be on a one-way trip, and not live to see the California poppies blowing in the breeze again. Every Marine was well aware of this, but each one knew in his heart it wouldn't be him that was killed in action in a place called Korea. No one ever thinks it will be him. If you didn't think that way, how could you ever hope to survive anyhow?

The Med cruise was like first-class on the Queen Mary compared to sea time to Korea. Below deck huge sleeping areas were jammed with troops. Cot-like bunks were rigged, one on top of the other, eight to ten high with barely enough room for a man and his gear.

The kid from New York summed up the upcoming ordeal best.

"The fucking D-train to Manhattan wasn't this crowded in the rush hour. Now we know how those fucking Pilgrims felt on the Mayflower."

The ship turned into little Las Vegas in no time. The Pacific Ocean had its share of sharks, as did the ship that plowed through those waters. Gamblers are like horse shit. They're everywhere, and they prowled that ship like hookers at Jack's Lighthouse looking for fast dollars.

Jack had learned the hard way about card games and shooting crap. He lost thirty bucks once about five minutes after receiving it in the pay line at Lejeune. That was two week's take home pay, and he never did it again. Marines would travel throughout the ship to various card games, and many guys sent hundreds of dollars home in money orders to be put aside for them. The Massachusetts crew saved whatever cash they had for one last liberty when they got to Japan.

Word had spread on what to expect on arrival in the Land of the Rising Sun. Salty Marines from World War II and China service passed the word over the years that Oriental women were different from others around the world. The tale went that the opening to their promised land ran sideways.

The Navy corpsman from Florida gave his professional opinion: "Pussy is pussy no matter what direction it takes."

The kid from New Orleans set the record straight with what sounded like the voice of experience.

"I shacked up with a beautiful Chinese lady in the back of a laundry she ran near Bourbon Street. Her eyes were beautifully slanted, but her path to paradise ran north and south. Don't expect anything different in Japan."

The crossing was miserable, and all hands were eager for one night of liberty in Kobe before going to Inchon, Korea, and whatever lay in store for them. They all headed out for Japanese beer … and whatever else they could find on a night on the town.

Chapter 37

In September of 1950, General MacArthur, the Commander-in-Chief of the Far East, called on the United States Marine Corps to do what they did so well in the Pacific during World War II. He planned an amphibious assault behind North Korean Lines at Inchon, the port for the city of Seoul, which was very close to the 38th parallel and the North Korean Army supply lines.

The Navy had to navigate a narrow channel with dangerous currents, while on the lookout for coastal battery sites. The attack caught the enemy by surprise, and in five days of house-to-house fighting, the Marines took over Inchon.

The bitter cold welcomed Jack and Al to the land they had been seeking for the past two years. Inchon was now the destination of replacement Marines from the States every month. It was crowded with men, supplies, vehicles, and a collection of broken down trains that would convey some of the troops north toward the 38th parallel.

Jack hated to say goodbye to Ron, who went by truck to join motor transport at the division level. When the going gets tough Ron was a guy you'd want close by. He would back down from nothing, and Jack would miss him.

Parting company with Al was like loosing a brother. Jack's orders were to join the 3rd Battalion, 7th Marines, and Al was headed for the 5th Marine regiment. Al had to wait for transportation, as the 5th Marines were in reserve. The 3rd Battalion 7th was at the 38th parallel on the main line of resistance, the MLR. Jack boarded the train with a heavy heart. He and Al tried to joke about the future, but they both knew the upcoming road wouldn't be as friendly as the one from Lejeune to Penn Station in New York.

The dilapidated train looked like something out of the Old West. The last time the heating system worked must have been when Jesse James and his brother Frank were raising hell in Dodge City. It felt like you were standing on the street corner at Tremont and Boylston on a zero-degree day with the wind coming across Boston Common.

As the train lurched north toward distant thunder-like sounds that had nothing to do with the weather, Jack thought back to the train at Yemessee and the cattle-car ride to Parris Island.

That short, frightful trip had actually set the stage for what lay in store during the months ahead.

The D.I.'s, in their own way, had planted the seeds in Jack Harrington's mind that he was prepared and had the balls to stand tall when it really counted. Lt. Trimble had taught him that surviving the ordeals that might arise was a matter of being prepared, and to never give up on yourself or the men you served with.

Two years ago he was a kid who really didn't know his ass from a hole in the ground about himself or what life was all about. Now, as a corporal in the Marine Corps heading into the real thing, he wasn't a kid anymore. He was more confident than ever that he would lead by example, as Lt. Trimble had always done. The lieutenant also said the race would be won by the guy with the most heart. Jack's was pumping a little faster than normal, but only to try and generate some heat in a body that was ready for the starting gun to go off.

The northbound train vibrated worse than an old truck on a washboard road, and the refrigerated cars were filled with the steamy breath of huddled-together Marines. Frostlike exhaust fumes from the waiting trucks hung in the air, and a buck sergeant read off the name and truck assignment of each Marine for the ride toward the MLR. Then, in his own way, he wished the new replacements well.

"Chesty Puller always welcomed the opportunity to engage in combat as it gives each Marine the chance to really earn all the fucking money the government pays us. Stay off the skyline. Semper Fi!"

Chapter 38

The Korean War had developed into its World War I phase. The trenches that ran for miles through the hills were reminiscent of what the troops had to contend with in 1917 Europe. The First World War was termed 'The war to end all wars', yet thirty-five years later men were once again wallowing in the trench lines trying to stay alive.

Reporting in to the Command Post bunker built into the reverse slope of the trench line was like entering the musty root cellar at the Boy Scout camp where Jack spent time as a kid.

"Welcome to the 7th Marines," grinned the kid from Pittsburgh. "You'll love it here. It's ten below fucking zero in the winter, and close to one hundred in the summer. This makes working in a steel mill seem like a vacation on the fucking Riviera. We try and sleep a little during the day, and crawl out of the bunkers and rabbit holes at night to go hunting for Luke the Gook."

Jack's first few days on line were spent at the company C.P. with the company commander of How Company and other officers and N.C.O.'s. His main responsibilities were to interrogate the patrol leaders when they returned from nightly runs on the other side of the wire. Many areas of the trench line had barbed wire strung and areas called 'gates', where patrols would leave to check out Gooneyland.

Jack's job was to find out if the patrols saw changes in the terrain, any gooks, how much incoming they might have encountered, did they have a fire fight, etc. All this information had to be relayed back to the regimental command unit.

The idea of leaving the MLR and heading out into no man's land was enough to up your heartbeat, or even raise your voice an octave or two. At this point Jack was champing at the bit to go on a patrol and see for himself what it was all about out in front of the wire. He approached a second lieutenant, who had played basketball for Princeton and was a real asshole, according to the guys.

"It's not for you to question your job description, Corporal. The Marine Corps has a plan, and your part of the plan is to gather information and report that information to people up the ladder of command," said Mr. Ivy League.

*This guy **is** an ass hole, thought Jack,* as he replied, "Sir, I've been trained to lead patrols, so I just thought it might make sense if I found out first hand what's happening outside the wire."

The second john just ignored him, and Jack shut his mouth.

As the sun was rising, Jack made his way to the head to take a piss before crawling into the sleep bunker. Members of the Korean Service Corps were just arriving with huge packs on their backs loaded with supplies. The KSC were older South Koreans who worked bringing supplies up to line and to the outposts in Gooneyland. Incoming had been coming in all night, but not too heavily. Sometimes Luke the Gook would throw in a huge barrage just as the sun came up, hoping to catch the troops a little off guard before sack time.

Jack had found out real fast that you don't have to be a fucking genius to figure out when incoming is going to be close. It had its own special sound when close, and if it's too close for comfort you don't hear a fucking thing … it's too late! Thanks to Lt. Trimble, he had already picked out a slight groove in the ground near the head, and was in the prone position, eating dirt.

The smell of cordite, mixed with the KSC being blown away, burned his nostrils. The screams of those still alive seared his brain.

Jack yelled, "Corpsman! Corpsman!"

He ran and tried to pull one of the Koreans into the area where he was. It was over in a flash. Three dead and two wounded, and the reality of what Jack had gotten himself into hit home, just as if Ronnie had kicked him in the balls!

Nothing prepares you for your first go around with death-dealing incoming. It's like nothing you can imagine in your wildest dreams. Somehow, when you were a kid watching the war movies, it always seemed glamorous and exciting … it isn't! The terrifying sounds, mixed with a dust storm of dirt, rocks, shrapnel and that unexplainable smell are embedded in your thoughts forever.

If those who decide that it's time to go to war were first forced to experience incoming and its agonizing results, there would be no wars!

Chapter 39

In the movie *Sands of Iwo Jima,* John Wayne played Sergeant Stryker, a tough as nails career Marine who took no shit from anyone. He always kept the troops out of the hot sun meaning, of course, that he always took care of the men in his outfit.

Well, Gunnery Sergeant Parker of H/3/7 could have played Sergeant Stryker, as he was the real thing. If you took toughness, courage, caring, an invincible attitude, dedication to duty and the Marine Corps, and poured it into the frame of a six-foot man … there would stand Gunny Parker! He was a career Marine who had served with honor in combat in the Pacific during WWII. The commanding officer of How Company was Captain McIntire, a career officer who had also served in combat on the Pacific Islands, and was a great leader.

"Harrington, quick thinking in helping out the KSC people," said Gunny Parker. "I understand you wanted to go in front of the wire yourself last night. If that's of particular interest to you, you may want to think about asking for duty with a line company, and let some other S-2 guy handle the paper work. We're always looking for a good fire-team leader, if you want to think about it. I'll put in a word with the captain, if you want."

Jack joined the 2nd platoon, How Company the next day, as the Gunny took care of the transfer.

The following night Jack went in front of the wire for the first time. A buck sergeant, Marc Randall, was taking a squad on patrol, thirteen men counting himself. Jack was the first fire-team leader, and was told to stay near the squad leader to learn the ropes on his first night out. Their orders were to check in by sound-power phone at three checkpoints ... Able, Baker, and Charlie ... and report, in a whisper, how things were going. At checkpoint Charlie, they were to set up an ambush and wait to see if any gooks tried to infiltrate the areas surrounding outposts that were set up in front of the MLR.

Lying still for hour after hour in freezing cold waiting for Luke the Gook is no fucking fun.

Randall beckoned Jack and whispered, "Sometimes when the wind is blowing toward you, you can smell the fucking gooks coming. They eat rice with fish heads and garlic, and when they're downwind and close, you'll know!"

No action – no incoming – no small arms fire – just a cold body that was glad to get back to the MLR that night!

Jack's fire team was made up of a PFC from Chicago, Donny Harris – a black kid, whose nickname was "Beebop" – a PFC from South Carolina, Harry Robinson – and a seventeen-year-old kid from Topeka, Kansas, Bill Dean Boyer. Each sleep bunker was equipped with a small, flat-top kerosene stove, which kept the bunker plenty warm so that with the help of a sleeping bag, you could sleep like a log. The strange thing was that even the incoming didn't wake you up, unless it was right on top of the bunker or in the trenchline nearby.

During the day one Marine would always be awake in the bunker as a 'fire watch', and the shift for each Marine was usually a couple of hours. The fire watch would also constantly check the trenchline, and look out on Gooneyland to be sure some crazy bastards didn't do any sneaking around in the daylight.

Jack worked with his fire team constantly. He reminded them to keep proper intervals on patrol, to always be a step ahead to pick out possible cover in case of incoming, to use sign language as much as possible on patrol, to keep the safety on their weapon on so that in case they slipped on patrol there wouldn't be the chance of pulling the trigger, … and to always make sure they had plenty of chow before going on patrol!

At their usual critique before going on patrol, Beebop said, "Jack, this reminds me of Snow White and the fucking seven dwarfs. She was always bugging those fucking dwarfs and taking care of them. She even had them whistling that fucking song as they went to work! By the way, how come the chick was called Snow White and not Snow Brown or Snow Black?"

They all laughed, but each guy, including Beebop, in a short period of time had come to know that Jack always had their best interests in mind, and they had great faith in him. When Jack would lead larger patrols, even though his fire team wasn't scheduled to go, they always volunteered if he needed them.

"Tonight's the night we bring Luke back to the MLR!"

The objective was to set up an ambush out in Gooneyland with the hope of getting a prisoner to send back to the rear to be interrogated. The plan was to wait for a gook patrol, make contact, and during the firefight throw a couple of concussion grenades that would daze at least one gook so he could be dragged back to the MLR alive.

The longer you wait out in no man's land, the more your mind and your eyes play games with you. At times you can see advancing figures in the darkness, then blink your eyes and there's nothing there. It takes great concentration and discipline to stay cool and figure out what's real and what isn't.

The combination of below zero weather, strong winds, and darkness made waiting for Luke to waltz into sight unsettling, to say the least.

"Jesus Christ!" whispered Bee Bop. "I smell fucking garlic pizza in the wind!"

To Jack, it was more like the Boston Fish Pier with fried garlic thrown in.

"Let the C.P. know we may be making contact, Harry. Tell 'em we're at checkpoint #3, and to stand by with the mortars. When the first gook gets to within twenty yards or so, we'll fire at the guys behind him. I'll hit the first fucker low in the legs, and throw the concussion grenade. We'll grab the son of a bitch and haul ass. As soon as we get him, call in the mortars, Harry!"

"Sounds good, Jack!"

Most plans never work out the way you think they will, and this one was no exception. There were at least a dozen gooks, maybe more.

"Fuck the prisoner! There are too many to fuck with. We'll kill 'em all and move out before they send incoming!" yelled Jack.

It seemed like it lasted forever, but it was less than a minute of continuous firing from both patrols. The gooks were completely surprised and unorganized as they were shattered with small arms fire.

183

"Call in the mortars, Harry, and let's haul ass!"

They reached the MLR without any casualties. The Chinese patrol had probably been wiped out from the firefight and mortar attack.

"No prisoners, Harrington?"

"No, Gunny. We were outnumbered, and the terrain didn't allow us to maneuver enough to get a prisoner without jeopardizing our entire patrol. I figured we were better off to wipe them out, and get a prisoner some other time."

"Good thinking, Harrington. Besides, it would have been a pain in the ass to ship that little fish-eating bastard back to Division!"

The 3rd Battalion had been on line for a number of weeks before Jack joined them, and were scheduled to be relieved and go back to reserve. The Gunny made the rounds, and his message was short and sweet:

"Leave these trenchlines and bunkers squared away! Other Marines will be living here, and we want their stay to be just as enjoyable as ours!"

Chapter 40

The reserve area was a welcome sight. Three hot meals a day, showers, clean clothes, and last, but not least … no incoming! However, life in reserve wasn't a vacation. Every day was filled with physical training, inspections, and the constant knowledge that you'd be back on line soon.

Rumors, or scuttlebutt, always ran high as to when the war would be over. Truce talks at Panmunjom reopened in late 1952. General Eisenhower, who was campaigning for President, vowed two weeks before election to bring the fighting in Korea to an end. His promise, if elected, was to visit Korea and see what was going on at the MLR.

Beebop Harris put it best when he said, "He might have been an okay fucking general, but now he's like every other politician … he's full of shit! His 'going to Korea' line will get him thousands of extra votes, but what the fuck good will it do for him to come over here? Hey, Jack, maybe he'll come out on patrol with us, and you can tell him to keep his fucking interval or one round will kill the whole fucking squad!"

Word from the States was that the stalemated combat situation in Korea had become a depressing, no-win situation. The war was unpopular, and, as a Marine in the chow line said, "The only people in the States that give a shit about this so-called fucking 'police action' are the ones that have kids over here!"

A month after Eisenhower's easy win in the election, he headed for Korea, and spent all of four days with his entourage touring the country.

A Navy corpsman said, "I wish the fuck he had come out to Vegas with us last month, and I don't mean the one with the gambling casinos! If he thought Omaha Beach was a bitch, let him take about 5,000 rounds of incoming in one night on an outpost the size of the infield at Yankee Stadium!"

That was the first time the outpost called 'Vegas' was mentioned … but, it wouldn't be the last!

Burt McConnell, a Navy corpsman from Pennsylvania, had been transferred to H/3/7, and was with the 2nd platoon. A good-looking, curly-haired blond, he was a great guy for many reasons. Burt was a wheeler-dealer, and had that certain knack of always being able to locate and confiscate the important things for life in reserve.

One-hundred-ninety proof medicinal alcohol is one of the great elixirs of all time! A canteen cup with an ounce or so of '190' and grapefruit juice or grape juice puts a couple of "zombies" to shame! If a '190' cocktail doesn't get the wheels turning and your dick shaking, you might as well walk out in front of the wire in broad daylight and kiss your ass goodbye!

Burt got it by the gallon from corpsmen in reserve permanently with the division medical group. He would trade a pint here and there for cases of Asahi beer packed in wooden boxes with each twenty-ounce bottle wrapped in a straw sleeve, extra food, fruit juice, cigarettes, and yes, a piece of ass!

Gunny Parker always said, "You can put a Marine on a so-called deserted island, but eventually he'll come up with a couple of beers, cigarettes, and a piece of ass!"

The little Korean villages with thatched huts and poor people who worked the rice paddies were mostly off limits, but that never stopped any Marine with a 'hard' on!

The shit had hit the fan on line, and the stay in reserve was going to be cut short. Along with the smell of spring came tons of melting snow, the thawing of the Imjim River, and Chinese communist troops ready to raise hell along the mountainous 33-mile MLR. Since October, when they had the shit kicked out of them on an outpost called 'The Hook', the Chinese had laid low and been content to run patrols and pour on the incoming.

The peace talks at Panmunjom continued, and the Chinese knew that if and when an armistice was signed, any territory they had captured would remain theirs. So, there was a method to their madness in escalating the war in the months ahead.

Stretched out in front of the MLR were outposts everywhere: Esther, Dagmar, Bunker Hill, The Hook, Boulder City, Berlin and East Berlin. Then, there were the Nevada cities: Carson, Reno, and Vegas. Typically, outposts were manned by a rifle platoon of forty men and two corpsmen, and heavily reinforced with weapons company men with machine gun sections and mortars. In the months ahead, some of bloodiest fighting of the war would result in over a thousand Marines being killed or wounded. The Chinese casualties included thousands known dead, and a regiment in tatters.

The three Nevada outposts were close to the 38th parallel, and about 10 miles from Panmunjom. Possession of the complete area gave whoever owned the real estate observation of the entire surroundings and positions of dominance.

As Jack said to the fire team, "Hey, ya don't have to be a fucking Rhodes scholar to figure out why Luke wants the fucking high ground! Both Reno and Vegas overlook Chinese rear area supply roads, and the Chinese can't make a move without Marines knowing what they're up to. To quote the Gunny: 'Stand by with your weapons at the ready, and don't take any fucking prisoners'!"

Chapter 41

Vegas was well over 500 feet high, and over 1,500 yards from the MLR, almost a mile. Getting to Vegas was almost as difficult as staying alive once you got there. Approaches to Vegas included large draws to the west and north, and a rear trenchline. Once you reached Vegas and climbed the hill to the top, you entered a trenchline system that ran for over 300 yards in more or less a circle around the outpost.

Some areas of the trench were about four feet deep, but deepened to about eight feet in other spots. The trench from the MLR was about five feet deep and two feet wide. Overhead fighting holes were dug into the trenchline, along with fighting holes with no overhead. Many rabbit holes were dug into the side of the trench, and two living bunkers and a warming bunker had been built. There was also a reinforced cave and a head.

A four-day rotation had been set up on Vegas, as after four days those still there were exhausted. Each evening wounded and dead were transported back to the MLR, and replacements arrived to take over. The KSC's arrived each night with supplies. During daylight hours, Marines stayed in rabbit holes or bunkers due to constant incoming and sniper fire. Getting any sleep was next to impossible because each time your eyes closed, incoming would jerk you to your senses.

H/3/7 headed for the MLR, and the 2nd platoon with Jack Harrington and his men moved out for Vegas. Arriving there, they were greeted by a sight that would stay in their minds forever. As they climbed the hill, the Marines they were relieving were leaving. No one spoke … they all had that blank, thousand-yard stare, and looked like zombies rising from the dead. Four days later, those men still on Vegas would look the same, as other troops took their place.

In four days the smell of cordite and that never to be forgotten 'meat market' odor of men being torn apart would be burned into everyone's memory, as thousands and thousands of rounds were delivered to Vegas by the Chinese. The second night on Vegas, two Marine replacements, one on each side of Jack, were blown into the air. The tremendous explosions killed the two, and Jack had a sharp, stinging feeling in his left thigh and cheek of his ass. Blood rushed from his nose and mouth, and his head exploded with the concussion of the shells. By some miracle, the stinging feeling was either from a flat piece of shrapnel or flying rocks. He'd be black and blue, but intact.

Burt, the corpsman, said he had a bad concussion and would have a headache for days.

The dead and wounded would be taken back to the MLR, and Jack told McConnell that he might as well stay with the platoon. The headache would go away in time, but not the memories.

During the day, incoming was the same as during the night – constant! A corpsman, not Burt McConnell, crawled out of his rabbit hole when he heard a cry for "Corpsman!" after rounds of incoming. There were other explosions, and Jack left his rabbit hole to help. There was the corpsman, with his body torn apart and the back of his head missing. His face, like a mask ready to be put on, was untouched and had a look of contentment about it.

Jack was in a frozen trance for what seemed minutes, but was only seconds, as he heard McConnell yell, "Get the fuck in the hole! We can't do a fucking thing for them now!"

The next night all hell broke loose. Chinese machine gun and small arms fire was heard, and mortar and artillery fire was increased toward Vegas. Hundreds of flares were fired out toward the Chinese hills, and the surrounding area lit up like a night baseball game. The Chinese wanted Vegas, and they were about to jump off in an effort to over run the outpost and take it for their own. Thousands of rounds of our artillery were sent screaming toward them, and the roar of rocket ripples went overhead toward the Chinese.

The rumor was that each set of rockets fired was equal to the cost of dozens of new Cadillacs. "Here come the Cadillacs!" was a welcome saying as the approaching roar was heard. This went on during the night, and the Chinese delayed the inevitable battle to take over Vegas.

Leaving Vegas alive was a miracle in itself. Jack would be on outposts Berlin and Boulder City in the future, but the recurring nightmares of Vegas would haunt him for years to come!

Chapter 42

A mile or so south of the MLR was an area equipped with showers, clean clothes, and hot food. Everyone that Jack had been with on Vegas, that survived, was in a state of semi-shock. There was little talk as they ate a hot breakfast, and prepared to join the rest of the battalion, who were still in reserve.

Jack and McConnell were sitting on a two-seater head like the old outhouses of years ago, when the sound of trucks straining to climb the hilly road was heard. The whirring sound was similar to incoming, and they simultaneously leaped out the door into a nearby ditch. As they lay in the hole with bare asses facing the sky, they looked at each other and laughed hysterically.

Harry Robinson, who had also survived Vegas, was making his way to the head when he saw Jack and Burt getting up from the prone position, while pulling up their pants.

In his best southern accent, he yelled, "I wish the fuck I had a camera! That fucking picture would make the cover of *Life* magazine – two combat Marines enjoying a little grab ass in Korea!"

After settling back in with the rest of the regiment in reserve, constant updates of the 'Nevada Cities' were given. Vegas had fallen to the Chinese, but the Marines had taken it back. From the time Jack's platoon had left Vegas to its' recapture, a total of over 500 Marine replacements had been sent out to Vegas, which was now termed 'the highest beach head in Korea'. Over a thousand Marines were wounded or killed. Chinese casualties were over 3,000.

The Commandant of the Marine Corps, General Sheperd, sent a dispatch to General Pollack, the leader of the 1st Marine Division:

"Have followed the reports of intensive combat in the 1st Division sector during the past weeks with the greatest sense of pride and confidence. The stubborn and heroic defense of Vegas, Reno, and Carson hills, coupled with the superb offensive spirit which characterized the several counterattacks, are a source of reassurance and satisfaction to your fellow Marines everywhere. On their behalf, please accept for yourself, and pass on to every officer and man of your command, my sincere congratulations on a task accomplished in true Marine fashion."

The message was read to all Marine outfits. At the same formation, Purple Hearts were awarded to those wounded during the past month. Knowing his parents would be notified, Jack wrote a fast note to let them know he was fine.

The Gunny said, "Harrington, all you need is two more of those hearts, and they'll ship your ass back to the States. You may get your chance sooner than you think … report to the company C.P. at 1300!"

The 7th Marines would be going back on line in a few weeks. They were to relieve a portion of an Army unit, and also some Turkish troops who manned a portion of the MLR in the same location. The Gunny wanted Jack to be part of an advance party to check out the area, and go on a patrol or two with Army personnel to become familiar with patrol routes. When more information was available, Jack would get the word. In the meantime, they continued to train, enjoy Asahi beer, '190', and were told a one-day trip to Seoul to raise a little hell would happen one of these days!

Each day a truck headed down the dusty, roller coaster road to Seoul with about a dozen guys for one day of R&R, rest and recuperation. It should have been called 'fuck your brains out day'. Seoul was a city of shacks and slums, and a bunch of bars with back rooms with cubicles, where Korean women spent the days and nights telling a different guy every ten minutes that he was 'Number fucking one!'

Jack and his fire team immediately went to a bar called The New Yorker, which was like comparing *The Ritz* in Boston with The International in Danvers. However, compared to the Seoul New Yorker, The International **was** like *The Ritz*! A few quick beers, and it was into the cubicle of love with a one-inch-thick mat on the floor. Next to jumping into a rabbit hole on Vegas, this was the fastest entrance and exit from a place of warmth you've ever seen! During the remainder of the day, the next couple of visits to the promised land took a lot longer ... maybe a total of two minutes!

Beebop put it best when he said, "Hey, we're not here to make a long lasting impression on some chick. We're here to get our rocks off a couple of times, and have a bunch of beers. If these new found friends aren't that good looking, just put a Marine Corps flag over their face and fuck for the Corps!"

The New Yorker somehow actually served hamburgers! No one asked what the burgers were made of, but with a lot of onions and ketchup, a number of beers, and a Miss South Korea telling us we were number fucking one, it was one hell of a day!

The following morning the Gunny said, "I hope you got your ashes hauled, Harrington. Now, you can concentrate on how those fucking doggies run a patrol. You'll be going up later today for a look see."

Chapter 43

The Turk's sector on the MLR was like the Newton town dump, but dirtier. There were C-ration cans in the trenchline, and the bunkers smelled like the inside of your locker at high school where you'd left a wet shirt and jock for a week. The Turks were wild looking bastards, and many had butcher-like knives on their gun belts. They gave Jack that 'What the fuck are you doing here?' stare. Jack gave them his best imitation of the 'Gunny Parker' stare, as he checked out the Turk area.

In the Army C.P., Jack listened to the game plan for the nightly patrol that he would go on. Much of the pre-patrol talk was similar to what he was familiar with. The patrol leader went over the checkpoints, four of them, on an overlay with patrol routes highlighted in red. They left the gate in the darkness, and headed toward the hills.

The patrol traveled much slower, and bunched up like Lt. Trimble pounded into his men never to do. Upon reaching the first checkpoint, the dozen men spread out a little and assumed the prone position. The Army sergeant called in that all was well at checkpoint Able, and that they would continue to checkpoint Baker. Well over an hour later, they were still at checkpoint Able when a message was sent back that they had reached their second objective.

Jack was stunned and confused as he crawled over to the patrol leader.

"What's going on?" he asked the sergeant.

The sergeant whispered, "You can run your patrols your way, and we'll run ours our way".

They spent the night at the first checkpoint, but reported in that they had reached the other three and all was quiet. Upon returning to the MLR, the critique in the C.P. was all bullshit. Jack was about to question the officers and patrol leader about the so-called battle plan of the patrol, but he decided to lay low. However, he did report the fucked up patrol information to the Gunny when he returned to H/3/7.

"It doesn't surprise me," said the Gunny, "but it's extremely dangerous to operate that way. False information is far worse than no information at all. What if some night that fucking patrol reported no gooks anywhere, and then they were able to infiltrate the supply trains or an outpost because these fuckups gave the all-clear signals.

"That's a court martial offense, and it's up to the captain to decide on how he wants to handle it with the dogfaces. It also puts added pressure on us to run patrols of the area as soon as we get on line. There are some good Army outfits, Harrington, but you sure as shit didn't find one of 'em!"

In two days, they were scheduled to take over the Army sector and a portion of the Turk area. Jack had found out through Burt McConnell, who had a corpsman friend with the 5th Marines, that some of the regiment had just come off line, and were a couple of miles away. Jack and Burt finagled a day off, and headed toward the 5th Marines. Jack's intent was to try and locate Al Garbetti, and Burt went along just for the hell of it.

It's a small world, and there was Al heading up a machine gun section in Weapons Company.

"Jesus Christ! Am I glad to see you!" they said in unison.

The afternoon was spent drinking Asahi beer, yelling laughingly for allowing each other to volunteer for duty in Korea, and talking about the so-called 'old days'. The Med cruise seemed as though it happened ten years before, although it was only a few months.

Before parting company, Burt gave Al the extra canteen he had brought along filled with 'white lightening' and told him to mix it about 10 parts juice to 1 part '190'. His time in reserve would pass at a much easier pace!

Words weren't necessary between Jack and Al. One look between them meant … "For Christ's sake, take care of yourself, and I'll see you real soon!"

Chapter 44

The trucks arrived, and H/3/7 loaded up for the dusty, hilly ride to the MLR. Jack made sure his squad, as he was the squad leader now, was set in the truck, and prepared to climb over the tailgate.

"Why don't you ride up front in fucking style?"

He'd never seen Ronnie Torrance before with such a smile on his face.

"Ronnie! What the hell are you doing here? I thought you'd be driving some fucking general around division headquarters!"

"I wish the fuck I was," said Ronnie, "but, at least when I drop you assholes off on line, I get the hell out of there while you eat dirt and dodge incoming!"

Nothing had changed with Ronnie ... he was still the same wild man. He explained that in a mile or two we would cross an area of almost half a mile called '76 alley'. The Chinese could see this section of the road, and would unload on us with mortars and 76 mm guns as we came into the open.

As we approached the alley Ron said, "I wish the fuck we had the Lincoln!" as he floored the truck.

Incoming was everywhere, and Ron did a hell of a job to keep the truck on the road. Some trucks were hit, but Ron got them past the open area without a hit.

The troops were dropped off about a quarter of a mile from line, to walk the remaining distance.

"Jack, you should see this truck fly through the alley when it's empty! It's a scary fucking ride, but in a weird way, exciting as hell! For Christ's sake, stay off the skyline! Good luck!"

They walked toward the MLR on each side of the road at the proper intervals as incoming commenced everywhere. It was like a movie … only the real thing! Gunny Parker walked down the middle of the road as if he was on liberty in Hollywood.

No panic, no hesitation, as he said, "We can't get caught on this fucking road! Keep your interval and move out on the double! Move it! Move it! Move it!"

For a second it reminded Jack of the train in Yemassee, and leaving it as fast as possible. They reached the reverse slope of the MLR, and took cover the best they could.

The Gunny yelled calmly, "When the shit stops hitting the fan, we'll move into our new home!"

They settled into the new sector, and went about the business of running patrols and trying to stay alive through the constant incoming.

Chapter 45

Jack's patrol had just reached their final checkpoint and were preparing to lie in wait for any enemy activity, when suddenly they received small arms fire from an area a hundred or so yards ahead to the left. There were muzzle blasts from a number of weapons, and they could hear the snapping of some rounds as they went overhead. There was also a spattering of rounds nearby, but no one was hit in the initial blast. They set up a small perimeter, and opened fire at the flashes.

When three fire teams open up there's plenty of fire power, as a Marine squad is equipped with three Browning Automatic Rifles (BAR's) that deliver one hell of a lot of rounds! That, combined with M-1's, is nothing to fuck with! They heard Chinese troops yelling through the fire, and called back to the C.P. for mortar cover. The forward artillery observer called for heavy artillery. In minutes, Luke the Gook got the shit kicked out of him! They were told to terminate the patrol and head for the MLR immediately, as a Chinese attack could be in the making.

A few hundred yards from the gate, the sky lit up with flares from Gooneyland … they were caught out in the open.

"Move out! Move out!" Jack yelled, as he urged the patrol past him and took up the rear with another suggestion to "Move the fuck out!"

They were surrounded by incoming, and Bill Boyer went down with a hit. Beebop helped get him over Jack's shoulder, and they made the final dash to the trenchline. They were sure Bill would be okay. There were no signs of a lot of blood, just a minor wound in the left shoulder, but he was unconscious. The squad thought perhaps the concussion had knocked him out. They brought him to a small aid station in the reverse slope area, and headed back to the trenchline.

Word came back later that Bill Dean Boyer had died. He had a small piece of shrapnel pierce his temple, and it killed him. The squad was devastated, as Bill, the quiet kid from Topeka, was a favorite. He had wanted to play professional baseball, and talked about the game all the time. Here was a seventeen-year-old kid, who would never fulfill any of his dreams, and Jack would never forget him. The episode left them all stunned for many days.

Sleep wouldn't come for Jack as he lay in the bunker. Thinking of Bill Dean Boyer not making it was almost too much to deal with. His thoughts switched to Carol and whether they would ever end up together. If they ever did, and had a son, they would name him Bill Dean. Jack knew Bill Dean Boyer would like that. He also knew how proud he'd be to have a Bill Dean beside him in years to come.

The Marine sniper was equipped with the Springfield 03 rifle with a fancy telescopic sight, and he loved his work! Just before daylight he would settle into a small, camouflaged crevice in front of the MLR, and zero in on a Chinese trenchline about a thousand yards away.

"No fucking way can you hit one of those sons of bitches from here!" Jack would joke with him.

"You only get to squeeze off one round, and then get back to the fucking trench fast," said the sniper, "but, I've been known to nail a few of those bastards!"

Jack loved the feel of the '03', and asked if he could fire it sometime.

"Some morning I'll give you a shot at Luke, if you want. This ain't like 600 yards at the rifle matches — but, you do have the scope and your target will look like it's right in front of you! You need some luck, though, because you never know about the wind. I always aim a little higher then I think I should.

"There's one area on the lower portion of that hill that ha^r a small bunker with a parapet. I've seen movement there n

211

times, and you can bet your ass those fuckers are looking at us just like we're looking at them!"

There was nervous excitement pumping through Jack's trigger finger, and he remembered what the major on the rifle range said: "Breathe slowly, don't rush, hold your breath, and squeeze ever so lightly!"

The scope was incredible! He had a bird's-eye view of the bunker when he squeezed off one round that he was sure hit the gook in the chest as he fell back.

"I'm telling ya," yelled Jack in the trenchline, "I nailed that fucker!"

"You may have or you may not have … but, if you didn't, you sure pissed them off! That fucking incoming wasn't for nothing!" said the sniper.

Jack woke up with a scream an hour later with a huge rat sitting just above him in the bunker.

"Those fucking Turks had so much garbage around here the rats thought they were in Heaven!" said Beebop.

Chapter 46

Jack had written a letter home before going back up on line, and mentioned that they were headed to the MLR near two outposts called Berlin and East Berlin. Outpost Vegas protected any enemy approaches to Berlin from the north and northwest, so that made Berlin fairly secure. Berlin, in turn, protected any enemy approaches from the north and northwest to East Berlin, making it fairly secure, too.

Losing Vegas to the Chinese had changed the whole fucking ballgame, as the Gunny said. The Berlins were wide open to the Chinese, and it was just a matter of time before the shit would hit the fan on both outposts. The Berlins were only 300 yards from the MLR, nearer than other outposts, and if Chinese troops manned these strategic positions, it could be a disaster.

Both outposts were under attack, and Jack's squad was sent out to Berlin to replace Marines killed and wounded in the action. The rain wouldn't let up, and the trench leading to Berlin had three to four feet of water in it, as did the trenches on the outpost. Berlin was smaller in area than Vegas, but had the same layout, more or less. Incoming was just about as heavy as on Vegas, and the constant rain made it even more difficult to man the outpost.

It's always hairy running patrols from an outpost, and usually they're sent out from the MLR. However, since the Berlins were so close to line, a patrol was sent out from Berlin to try and check on what the Chinese were doing. With Vegas close by, and manned by Chinese, you never knew what you might run into.

Jack took a squad out the first night they were on Berlin. It was tough going because of the ongoing rain, poor visibility, and mud everywhere. Fortunately, there was no contact with the Chinese, and upon returning to Berlin, Beebop wondered aloud, "What fucking genius officer decided running patrols from the outpost was a good idea?"

The following day the rains continued, and the incoming was almost as heavy as the rain. Crammed into a bunker, it was next to impossible to get any sleep, so most of the talk was about possible R&R in Japan. A Marine 'short timer', who had only a few weeks left before heading back to the States, told us what we all wanted to hear.

"You get to the R&R center in Kyoto and you shower, shave, and get clean, starched khakis. You go through the pay line, and draw out a couple of hundred bucks. Then, you listen to some asshole tell you how to behave on your five days of R&R, which, of course, goes in one fucking ear and out the other. You go to the gate of Camp Fisher, and outside that gate is pussy everywhere! It's like the fucking cattle auction back in Oklahoma. You check out the stock, and put your brand on your new love for five days!

"You head for Hotel Happy, and have beers up on the roof with hundreds of other jarheads and their 'girlfriends'. You check into one of the hotels and get laid real fast, then take a hot bath while Miss Congeniality sponges you like a baby. You get laid again, take another bath, and blink your eyes ten fucking times to make sure you're not dreaming! You hit all the nightclub/bars in the city, you have a glow on for five days, and you dip your wick as often as you want.

"On the fifth fucking day, you think very seriously of going to the commanding officer of Camp Fisher and asking permission to marry Miss Japan. Then, you remember that she has been doing this for a couple of years with other assholes just like you! You give her a huge tip, and thank her and tell her you love her, and she says the same. You both know it's bullshit, but you've had one hell of a week, and hope like hell the war is over before you get back to your outfit!"

The only sound during his explanation of R&R was the incoming outside the bunker, as everyone was fascinated with what lay in store for them, hopefully soon.

Then, Harry Robinson said, in his southern drawl, "Somebody told me Japs don't give blow jobs. Is that true? I mean, what the fuck, if they don't smoke the White Owl, the fucking week is a waste of time!"

"Let me tell you guys this," said the R&R veteran. "They've heard the second part of the biggest lie in the world, 'the check is in the mail', and 'I won't come in your mouth' from every fucking Marine who comes to Japan. Be happy to just fuck your brains out because Miss Japan will give you the standard answer, 'No suckie dickie'!"

A Marine in the bunker said that thoughts of Kyoto would be with him and his squad on patrol that night, as they were all brought back to the present time with a huge explosion on the roof of the bunker. The patrol, however, was canceled because strange motor noises were heard in the early evening from the direction of Vegas. It sounded like trucks pulling in and out with supplies or troops.

Later in the night, the Chinese made assaults on the Berlins. They came from Vegas, and the battle went on for three hours or so. Marine mortars, plus artillery illumination and tanks, played a huge part in stopping the assaults. Small arms fire from the outposts, along with machine gun fire, kept the Chinese from reaching the trenchline. Nine Marines were killed, and over 125 were wounded.

Chapter 47

The torrential rains continued and the trenches remained filled with three or four feet of water, especially the long trench back to the MLR. In the heavy rain, a patrol left Berlin to check on any possible Chinese movement out there in no man's land. Somehow, in the mud and rain, they veered slightly off the patrol route and entered a minefield. Either the mines had lain dormant during the winter months and suddenly come to life with the warm weather, or the minefield had recently been relaid.

The field was loaded with Soviet antipersonnel mines with both pull fuses and tension fuses, something the Marines had never seen before. In the heavy rain and mud, the Marines slipped around the field, and the results were devastating. Four Marines were killed and eight wounded, as mines exploded everywhere.

Back on Berlin, Jack heard the explosions and screams from Marines being blown apart. He and another Marine immediately left the outpost and headed for the sounds of Marines calling for help. The patrol leader, Sgt. Randall, was in the middle of everything helping the wounded. One Marine was caught up in some barbed wire and both of his legs were gone. He died as Jack tried to untangle him from the wire. All Jack knew was that his name was 'Tex', and he had stopped screaming.

They carried two wounded Marines out of the minefield, as others came to pull them back to the outpost. A flash went through Jack's mind of Lt. Trimble and his constant hammering about not bunching up. If more than one or two men entered the minefield, they were sure to slip and slide and set off more mines. He also knew that at any minute the Chinese would realize what was happening, and light up the area and throw in a shitload of incoming.

"I'll drag the wounded out first. You guys stay, and as I get them out, take off for the outpost with them," ordered Jack.

One of the wounded Marines set off another mine, and was killed as Jack and the other Marine traversed the minefield getting the wounded out. They then pulled the dead Marines out, and planned to bring them back to Berlin later that night, or the next night, if necessary.

Back on the outpost a corpsman, Jack, and others worked on the wounded, and prepared to navigate the trenchline back to the MLR with them. One Marine slipped from their grasp and sank in four feet of water. They literally had to go under water to pull him up. The incoming from the Chinese had begun, which made it all the more difficult to manipulate through the flooded route to the MLR. Jack received a tear in his left hand from a small piece of shrapnel, which a corpsman later took care of.

As always, the Marine Corps will go through hell to retrieve dead comrades from any situation. The four dead Marines were brought back to the MLR the following night. That same night, Harry Robinson was hit in the shoulder and upper arm.

As he was about to be transported back to the MLR by KSC members, Jack said, "Harry, stay out of the fucking hot sun!"

Harry, with his sly smile, said, "Jack, I'll live to piss on your grave!"

They both laughed, and Jack had a feeling inside of great closeness to the Marines he served with.

They were relieved of duty on Berlin by another forty or so Marines, and went back to the MLR. Two days later all hell broke loose as Luke decided fun and games were over. They were going to add the Berlins to their chain of outposts. The Chinese struck East Berlin first, where three dozen Marines manned the post, then Berlin where four dozen men were dug in. The small number of Marines was over run by hundreds of Chinese, and the outposts were lost.

The outposts and MLR received over 3,000 rounds of incoming, sometimes at the rate of one round per second. Early in the morning, word was passed along the MLR that at 0730 an all out assault would jump off from the MLR and retake the Berlins. At first, the Marines to be involved thought it was some kind of joke.

"Nobody in their right fucking mind would jump off in broad daylight to knock those motherfuckers off those fucking outposts!" yelled Beebop.

"Your key words are 'right fucking mind'!" said the college kid from Maryland. "Maybe some asshole general getting laid in Japan was told we lost the Berlins. Before he stuck his dick back in, he sent the order to 'Have those fucking Marines take those hills back at sunup'!"

Gunny Parker summed it all up as he walked the trenchline checking on the troops: "Do you fucking people want to live forever?"

As it started to get light, Jack checked his squad, and each of them had that calm but knowing look ... that this was probably absolute suicide. The amazing thing was that everyone was ready to attack.

Jack thought back to boot camp when a D.I. screamed, "When I say shit, you don't question me! You squat, and say, 'Sir! What color, Sir?' Do you understand me?"

222

"Sir! Yes, Sir!"

Then, Beebop broke Jack up with, "Jack, after we drive those motherfuckers off those hills, let's go back to Seoul and pat some ass!"

No one spoke as it was getting close to jump off time. In later years, tears would roll down Jack's face as he watched the movie *Gallipoli*, an Australian movie about the Boer War. The troops waited in a trenchline to jump off and take a hill, and the mission was sheer suicide. The men were all blown away, as word to cancel the assault came too late.

The retaking of the Berlins was canceled less than half an hour before zero hour. Jack read in later years that a recommendation had been made earlier about a possible readjustment of the whole sector, as the feeling was the Berlins could never be held for any length of time should the Chinese decide to put pressure on them. The opinion was that the outposts had gradually lost their value because between the MLR and the outposts, minefields, barbed wire, etc., their reinforcement and the counter attacks were too costly.

General Bruce C. Clarke, U.S.A., the I Corp commander, hit the nail on the head when he said, "Holding poor real estate for sentimental reasons is a poor excuse for undue casualties!"

Every Marine involved in the retaking of the Berlins is indebted to the general, for many of them would have died during that morning in July of 1953!

Chapter 48

Jack awoke to the corpman's announcement that the pleasure cruise was just about over.

"You'll be on land in a few hours. There's no incoming, no trenches, just cold beer and wild women!"

The naval hospital in Yokosuka was immense, and there were hundreds of wounded Marines there, as well as men from other service branches and many foreign countries. In Jack's ward on the second day at the hospital, he met a Marine from South Boston. John Driscoll hadn't been wounded in Korea. He was stationed in Yokosuka on guard duty at the hospital.

On one of his nights on the town, he had been involved in a bar room fight, and split his right hand badly when he decked some sailor with a shot to the jaw. John was on the Marine boxing team in Japan, and Jack imagined he and Ronnie taking on a dozen guys and kicking the shit out of them!

John knew all the Marines that pulled guard duty at the hospital, including those who manned the main gate. He and Jack were both confined to the hospital, and liberty was out of the question until they were cleared by the doctors.

However, when John said, "Let's go out tonight for a few beers and a piece of ass. I can get us through the gate with no problem, and I know some Japanese women you'd flip over. Just tell them you'll take then back to the States with you, and they'll treat you like you were that fucking ego maniac, General MacArthur!" … Jack was ready to move out!

True to his word, they passed through the gate like shit through a goose, and hit the night club scene. The clubs were wild … music, women, and always some kind of fight during the evening between the different services.

Jack gave John the message loud and clear.

"John, let's mind our own fucking business. We don't want anything to do with the Navy shore patrol, and I don't want to open up any of these stitches. Besides, I'm a lover, not a fighter!"

Jack thought back to Oran, Algeria, and Al Garbetti. Through their laughter, Al had told Jack that although he thought he was a great lover, he was actually the original 'minuteman'!

Jack had said, "Yeah, but think about how many times a 'minuteman' gets laid in an hour!"

A girl named Miki asked Jack if he wanted to dance. She was under five feet tall, and truly looked like a beautiful Japanese doll … no, not a Chinese doll! The age-old line of bullshit ran immediately through Jack's horny mind, *"What's a beautiful girl like you doing in a place like this?"* But, this time it was true! This girl was like the most beautiful girl in high school that you were afraid to talk to, and when you finally had the balls to do so, you stuttered!

They danced, and then sat at a small table and talked between dances and a few beers. She spoke English fairly well, at least to the point that they understood each other. To Jack, this was no 'wham, bam, thank you, ma'am' deal. He was actually nervous about asking to go wherever she took other 'minutemen'! Driscoll urged him to bring Miki along with him and another girl, but Jack said he'd wait for him in the bar. After an hour or so, Jack left some money with Miki, and asked if he could meet her the next night.

As he walked back to the hospital, he thought what a dumb shit he was. Then, he laughed to himself as he heard in his mind what Al Garbetti would have said.

"You've got the chance to bang some hooker that doesn't look like a hooker, and all of a sudden you become Father Flanagan at Boy's Town! I'm disappointed in you, Jack … you let your brain overrule your dick! You're a dumb shit!"

Jack's first thought the next morning was to see Miki that night, and Driscoll told him it would be no problem to go through the gate. Every morning the doctors made their rounds of the wards and checked on each Marine. The story on Jack was that he would be ready to leave in a couple of weeks.

Chapter 49

Jack had received a letter from his mother. Practically the minute he boarded the hospital ship in Korea, he had written a fast note to let them know he was okay and being well taken care of. His mother told him about the frantic time they had when the Boston newspaper headlines told of the Berlins being overrun by Chinese with huge Marine casualties.

She had called Al's mother to see if she had heard from Al, which she had. Mrs. Garbetti had then called all the relatives in Tuckahoe, and they said novenas at church for Jack. The prayers of so many people must have played a big part in pulling Jack through some of the ordeals he was involved in.

His mother then wrote about the Western Union deliveryman who had come to the door with a telegram stating Jack had been wounded. He had just delivered one with news of the death of another Marine who lived in Boston. The man was afraid to hand the telegram to Mrs. Harrington until she said, "Don't worry, we just had a note from our son telling us he had been wounded again, but is alright." They both had tears in their eyes on the front porch of the house.

A second note home from Jack told about heading to the hospital in Yokosuka, Japan, and Mrs. Harrington had passed that news along to Jim Emery.

"Harrington, you have a call from the States in the Medical Office," said the corpsman.

It was Jim Emery calling from Mac's Sunoco station in Newton Highlands! When the operator told Jim to deposit many dollars in coins, it took what seemed like ten minutes for the final quarter to drop into the phone box.

Jack's first question was, "For Christ's sake! Is Chuck Phinney with you?"

Jim laughed as he said, "No, you asshole! These are my own hard earned quarters!"

Jack couldn't believe Jim had called from the States, and it was one of the best surprises of his life. Jim closed with a promise that the convertible would be at his disposal when he returned.

"You can put the top down, and drive over to Richard's Drive In for a burger, then head for The Last Chance. Who cares if it's the middle of winter!"

Much time was spent with Miki, and Jack had to keep in mind what Al had always told him about himself. *"You fickle son of a bitch. Don't make any long term commitments because you'll change your mind the next day when another girl smiles at you!"*

There were also two Marines on permanent duty in Japan with Driscoll, who were trying to get permission to marry Japanese girls. There was a lot of red tape involved, and it was next to impossible to work it out.

A salty Navy chief put it best at one of the 'before liberty' talks he gave Marines before their first night on the town after being in the hospital.

"You jarheads always think with your dicks, but before you fall in love with the first steady piece of ass you've ever had, remember this: When you're dating Miss Lovely, every time you get laid put fifty cents in a jar. Then, when you marry Miss Lovely, every time you punch the cushion, take out fifty cents. It will take you seven and a half fucking years to get those coins out of the jar! So, for someone who thinks with his dick, it makes no sense to put that kind of restriction on your Johnson!"

Miki had gone out to the country to visit her parents, so Jack had a night of drinking beers and talking about going back to the States. After many bottles of Asahi the conversation got louder, and a swabbie at the next table made the mistake of commenting on Driscoll's Boston accent.

"I CAN'T HEAR YOU !"

"You sound like you just got off the turnip truck from some foreign country!"

Laughter came from the group of sailors, as another one said, "All seagoing bellhops have speech problems!" More laughter.

"The last belle I hopped was your fucking sister, you New York cock sucker!" screamed John, as he pounced on the sailor, smashing his face into the deck.

The other sailors jumped on Driscoll, and Jack entered the 'ring' thinking, "Here go the stitches!"

The Shore Patrol arrived, and the two Marines were escorted back to the hospital, facing charges of unauthorized liberty and, perhaps, assault.

Chapter 50

At 0800 the following morning, Jack Harrington was escorted into the office of the Executive Officer of the hospital, a Navy commander.

"Sir! Reporting as ordered, Sir!"

"Corporal! At ease, and please sit down," said the commander quietly.

Then, Jack listened for what seemed forever.

"I'm sure last night wasn't the first time you've arranged to, let's say, visit the surrounding area without being invited to do so. I have some of your records here, and what with being wounded three times, and seeing the war up too close, in many ways I don't blame you. However, we are running a huge hospital here, and trying to give the best care possible to men like you, and many who may never leave this facility because of wounds received.

"From your actions in Korea, you must be a leader of men, but you've set a poor example of that for your fellow Marines here at the hospital. They expect more from you, and so do we. Although you may not think so, we, in the Navy, are extremely proud of the way the Marine Corps handles adversity. Our corpsmen serving with you Marines always report about your extreme courage and dedication to duty.

"You've been through enough turmoil in the past few months, Corporal. I don't intend for you to have to face charges of A.W.O.L. or assault. I've talked to the staff, and your stitches are ready to be removed. That will be done today or tomorrow. Your stay here with us is over, and you'll be transferred to Camp Fisher in Kyoto. I'm sure within a few weeks or a month, you'll be heading back to the States. I, personally, don't want an incident of this kind to blemish your fine record, Corporal, and I wish you well in the future.

"By the way, I understand your confrontation was caused in part by comments on your manner of speech. I attended Harvard Medical School, and I'm sorry to say that you Bostonians do have a strange way of conveying your thoughts!" A slight smile crossed the commander's face as he asked if Jack had anything to say.

Jack took a deep breath, and fought back tears. There was no bullshit in what had been building up in his mind.

"Sir, I apologize to you and all the wonderful people who have helped me. The medical staffs on the *Repose* and here at the hospital are just the greatest. When corpsmen report about the courage of the Marines, we triple that statement for corpsmen that serve with us. I can't imagine doing what they do, and the way they do it. The true heroes of the Korean War are Navy corpsmen!

"I shall always remember your fairness, Sir, and concern for all Marines. In my case, it's extremely important for me to have a clean record in the Marine Corps, just for my own satisfaction of doing the job the way it should be done. My father attended Harvard, Sir, and he took me to a number of football games at the stadium. He always told me that in Harvard athletics, fairness to your competitors was far more important than winning the game. I can see, Sir, that the Harvard Medical School instills the same spirit in their doctors. I thank you, Sir, and you're probably right … we do talk funny!"

Jack visited Beebop, and they vowed to look each other up when they were on the 'outside'. You know, those 'keep in touch' promises come from the heart at the time, but never seem to turn out. The commander had helped John Driscoll through his little problem with the Navy, too, and John said he'd say goodbye to Miki for Jack after he did what he always wanted to do with her.

Final advice from John was, "Don't fuck up at Camp Fisher! They have one of the worst brigs in the Marine Corps. A gunnery sergeant runs it, and they say he makes D.I.'s seem like your nice old grandmother!"

They also vowed to have a number of beers at Blinstrub's in Southie!

Jack headed for the train station.

Chapter 51

Camp Fisher was like Grand Central Station in New York … busy as hell, with everyone in a hurry to get somewhere. Camp Fisher, of course, was every Marine's dream on the MLR. That's where R&R waited, along with women, booze, and five days of no incoming!

Jack was sent to Casual Company, where Marines awaiting transfer to the States put in their time. They were put to work in various jobs handling the troops coming in from Korea. A truce in Korea had been worked out soon after the *Repose* left for Japan. However, troops would remain on rotation for R&R for months to come.

Jack's job was to address a few dozen Marines at a time with a fifteen minute spiel on the 'DO NOTS' during their stay in Kyoto. He always began his talk by stating he had served with H/3/7 up until a few weeks before the war ended, and had just arrived himself from the Yokosuka Naval Hospital. He knew if he didn't, every one of the Marines would think he was an office pinky in Japan during the war, and didn't know shit. They weren't going to listen to him anyway, but at least they'd know he was one of them!

He always ended his session with the warning John Driscoll had given him.

"The brig here makes the Portsmouth Naval Prison look like shacking up at the Beverly Hills Hotel. I've never been a guest, but I'm told by many it's on the top of the list of bad ass places. Don't treat any Japanese woman badly! Don't punch any fucking civilians, or any other jarheads for that matter! Whatever you do, don't fuck with the Shore Patrol!

"You're all sitting there champing at the bit to get laid, and think I'm full of shit. Well, I am full of shit, but not when it comes to warning you about the brig. There have been guys never heard from again after entering that resort! So, … I warned you! Semper Fi! Enjoy yourselves!"

Three Marines from H/3/7 arrived for R&R.

One, a staff sergeant, said, "We knew fucking 'A' you wouldn't last long on the hospital ship! Hey, you were written up for a Silver Star for rolling around in that fucking minefield, and so was Randall. Some asshole sitting on his fat ass back at division will probably break it down to Bronze Star, if that. Good job, though! How's the pussy on R&R?"

"You know what the man says, Sarge. Has there ever been a bad one?" smiled Jack.

The next morning at chow seven prisoners, who had been locked up the night before, were marched in. One of them was from How Company. Jack left the chow line, and headed toward the prisoners, who would sit at attention at a table separated from everyone else.

As Jack caught the Marine's eye, and was about to say "What the fuck happened?", a Marine guard stuck a riot gun in his side.

"One fucking word out of you, and you'll join these shitbirds and pull brig duty longer than they will! Move out!"

Jack wanted to wrap the shotgun around his neck, but knew he wouldn't see the light of day until Gunny Parker retired from the Corps, and that was twenty more years!

Four days later, Jack saw the other H/3/7 guys, and asked what had happened. It turned out the guy got all greased up, and had a run in with a Jap at Hotel Happy. One thing led to another, and he threw the Jap through a bass drum in the band! Then, he stomped on him, and before they could get him out of there, the Shore Patrol grabbed his ass. Jack hadn't seen the Marine since the morning he almost joined him for a not-so-pleasant breakfast, and he didn't go back to Korea with the others.

In the months ahead, a military investigation was held in regard to brutality at the Camp Fisher brig. The word was that many of the guards, and the brig warden, were sent to the States and naval prison. Their stay couldn't have been too enjoyable when the word about who they were was passed along to the other guests!

Chapter 52

Checking over the list of incoming Marines headed for R&R was like opening your favorite present on Christmas morning. There, in bold print, was **ALBERT J. GARBETTI!** Jack's thoughts flashed back to the transfer list from Parris Island at Camp Lejeune ... Big Al was going on R&R!

"Jesus Christ!" they said in unison. "Am I fucking glad to see you alive!"

Jack quickly filled Al in on what had gone on, and Al did the same. Then, they got down to serious discussions on what places of interest Al should visit in Kyoto!

Al and another Marine, Bob Lawton, from the Boston area, served together on line. They each hit the gate, picked out a 'Miss Congeniality' for the week, and headed for the Hotel Happy rooftop to have a number of beers before Jack joined them. They spent a couple of hours drinking and bullshitting, and then Al said

241

he'd like to spend more time with Jack, but his dick told him it was time to saddle up and ride the trail to the promised land.

He left, towering over his new Japanese companion, who giggled as Al said, "I'm in love with you already!"

Jack's parting words were, "You fickle fuck!"

Four days later, Al and Bob appeared back at the base, and prepared to head back to Korea. They were in rough shape, exhausted, and half in the bag. The troops had changed back into combat issue, and all went to the mess hall for a complete chicken dinner before loading into trucks to go to the airport for the short hop back to Korea. Both Al and Bob sat leaning against the wall, passed out from booze and lack of sleep. When their names were yelled out at roll call, Jack answered for both of them.

Before they were, literally, loaded into a truck, Jack went into the galley where one of the cooks wrapped up two small, roasted chickens for him. He placed one each inside Al's and Bob's field jacket, buttoned the jackets, and hoped they would enjoy the treat when they came to!

Chapter 53

The Military Air Transport plane loaded up with some freight, and Marines being rotated back to the States. Among them was Jack Harrington, who felt he had been gone for years, although it was only nine or ten months. They would have a one-day layover at Hickham Field in Hawaii, and then head for San Francisco and Treasure Island for eventual discharge from the Marine Corps. During the long flight, there was plenty of time to daydream, reminisce about the past three years, and think about what might lie in store over the months ahead.

The indoctrination to war had left Jack in an extremely nervous state. He was jumpy, and never completely relaxed. Yet, in many ways, he was glad he and Al had continued their requests for duty in Korea. In all the Marine training, it was stressed that everything was geared toward insuring success in combat. Many times he had thought of what actual combat was really like, and how he would react to it. He learned that nothing in his future would ever test his courage or ability to make life-saving decisions like his tour in Korea.

He learned, too, that 'Semper Fi', always faithful, had nothing to do with being faithful to your country or fighting for your country, as you always saw in the old war movies. When the shit hits the fan, you respond for only two reasons: to survive and to help your fellow Marines survive. Being with men in the most trying circumstances, and witnessing the courage, sense of humor, and true caring for one another, is something that would come to the forefront in Jack's mind thousands of times during his life.

He now knew firsthand how incredible the accomplishments of the troops in World War II were. For men in the Pacific and European war zones to go through campaign after campaign for a number of years is one of the true wonders of the world, as far as Jack was concerned.

In his final days on the hospital ship, Jack had had a burning fear of going back to the MLR. He'd come close to being killed on so many occasions, and seen others killed, that the thought of once again testing his luck and sanity was constantly on his mind. Yet he knew that if, for some reason, the men he served with somehow called for his help, he would join them without a second's hesitation.

Learning about himself, and how he reacted to real adversity, would always give Jack a feeling of inner pride that he could never explain to anyone. It was just there, and even though a lot of heartache was involved, he was glad he had served.

Jack closed his eyes, and remembered what the Gunny always said: *"Whenever you have the chance, get some shuteye, for the time will come when you wish the hell you did!"*

Chapter 54

Reminders of 1941 were everywhere at Hickham Field. Although it had been twelve years since the Japanese bombed Pearl Harbor and did a job on surrounding bases, including Hickham, there were obvious Japanese fingerprints left behind. Chunks of stucco knocked out of buildings from bombings and strafing runs hadn't been replaced … perhaps, left as they were to remind those who passed through that nothing is ever completely safe from aggressors.

Jack wondered how long the remnants of war would remain in Korea. The trenches, bunkers, and completely treeless and vegetation-free outposts would be a silent monument to those who served, and to the over 34,000 U.N. troops who died in the three year war, along with over 100,000 wounded. Marine casualties totaled over 24,000 wounded and more than 4,000 killed.

That night most of the Marines paid a visit to the base slopchute. Jack drank too many beers, but with each guzzle he'd toast those he served with in Korea. That required that he have at least a dozen bottles! No one was left out, and he hit the sack late for a couple of hours of sleep before leaving for the States.

They arrived at Treasure Island, the naval base in San Francisco Bay, to go through processing. Some Marines would be transferred to other duty stations. Some, like Jack, were processed for discharge back to civilian life.

There was a tearful phone call to his mother and father to let them know he was being discharged, and then a call to Mrs. Garbetti to set her mind at ease about Big Al. Carol, who was at Stanford, was practically speechless when she heard his voice, and then she couldn't stop talking. Plans to meet in San Francisco were set up, and would be finalized in a day or two.

Then, as he had promised, Jack called Carmen Manero.

"You son of a bitch! I knew you'd be okay! Where are ya?"

"Treasure Island in San Francisco. I'll be out in a couple of weeks. I'll fly to New York, then Boston. Maybe we can have a couple of beers."

"We'll have more than a couple of beers for Christ's sake! Is Carol still in California?"

"I'm seeing her this weekend in San Francisco."

"Listen to me, Goombah. Stay at *The Fairmont Hotel.* You'll love the place, and have the same deal as New York. Don't give me any bullshit about it. The place will be yours. Call me when you know your flight number to New York. Bruno and I will pick you up. Stay over at least one night before going up to that fucking Beantown!"

Part of the weeks ahead would be spent listening to re-enlistment talk … 'Shipping Over' talks, as they were called. Jack had never given any thought to making a career of the Marine Corps. All he could think of was to get on a plane, and fly to Boston. There were promotions and cash bonuses in line for some who stayed in. Jack was also told that perhaps he'd have the opportunity of going to Quantico, VA, to O.C.S. … Officer's Candidate School … with 2nd lieutenant bars awarded upon graduation. The officer who interviewed him had been an enlisted man in the 6th Marines at Lejeune, and painted a pretty picture. A major met with Jack to give a final pitch for being a career Marine, officer, or enlisted man.

"Sir, I'm sure my tour of duty in the Marine Corps will be one of the highlights of my life. Where else would I have met men from all over the country, and be part of the finest fighting force in the world? Every issue of *Reader's Digest* includes a short story on unforgettable characters. I've met enough to fill the magazine for many years to come.

"I'm not sure what I'm going to do when I get out, but I think I'll work toward entering college and take it from there. It has been a great privilege for me to serve, and I'll always be proud to say I was in the Marine Corps. When all my processing is complete, Sir, I'm going back to Boston to civilian life. Being considered for O.C.S. is an honor. Being a career NCO would be, too, but I've decided to accept my discharge and move on.

Thank you, Sir!"

Chapter 55

Jack was welcomed to *The Fairmont* just like he was to *The Plaza*. The comfort of the suite was doubly welcome considering where he had been and what he had lived through over the past year. Seeing Carol standing in the doorway sent a feeling of huge relief through Jack.

It was the same feeling he always had when he made it back to the MLR after a nightlong patrol. You were glad to be back, but felt like you were going to cry like a baby. You never did, but, before falling asleep in a darkened bunker for a few hours, you almost wished you could.

Standing in the room hugging Carol was as if the emergency valve for your emotions was set off adjusting the pressure that had built up over the past few months. Not a word was said as Jack cried uncontrollably. They just sank into a couch, and held each other. Hours later after showering together, and then showering again after the complete relaxation that lovemaking brings, they went to Fisherman's Wharf for sightseeing and dinner.

The small, gold, four-leaf clover necklace that Carol wore winked at Jack from across the table.

"You bought this for me so I wouldn't forget you, as if I ever would," smiled Carol. "The rest of our little savings account is in my pocketbook. We can live like millionaires over the weekend, or save it for Christmas back in Boston. I'll be home for the holidays, and we'll spend a white Christmas together."

They both wished they could stay in the Honeymoon Suite at *The Fairmont* forever, but the thought of being together at Christmas was enough to make their goodbye one of great anticipation toward seeing each other back on the East coast.

Chapter 56

Every morning before reveille, Jack looked out the squad bay window to San Francisco Bay and Alcatraz prison. Each time he'd think of the brig at Camp Fisher, and that miserable fucking guard with the riot gun. Perhaps, at some time in the future, those sadistic bastards would run into the prisoners they tormented, and, hopefully, payback time would be a bitch!

As the Gunny always said, when the Chinese delivered an extra special load of incoming, "Don't get mad! Get even!"

Processing was delayed for Jack, as he had many physical exams due to his wounds. He was told that the two concussions could very well cause headaches and trauma for many years, and it was suggested that he go through a number of medical tests. Doctors and corpsmen advised him not to sign release papers until a disability percentage was awarded by the medical team, and that would take additional time.

For some reason, Jack didn't leave Treasure Island to go on liberty in San Francisco. He went to the slopchute on base each night, constantly thought of his friends who had been killed, and became more and more depressed about being delayed at Treasure Island. He would forego the red tape of all the medical hassles, and sign his release papers to receive his honorable discharge from the Marine Corps.

As he sat with his seabag in the Marine Corps bus heading for the main gate, he thought to himself ... *It's been a long fucking way from Yemassee to Vegas and the main gate heading to San Francisco. He had stayed off the skyline as much as possible, carried clean socks, kept his weapon clean, never bunched up, and always kept the troops out of the hot sun! Lt. Trimble was right. When the fucking gun goes off, forget about all the strategy and run as fast as you can! Maybe he'd just do that for the next fifty years, and see what happens at the finish line!*

Chapter 57

Carmen had added a few pounds to his huge frame, and now reminded Jack of 'Crusher Casey' with a New York accent. Crusher was the king of wrestling at the Boston Arena, and when he got an opponent in his famous bear hug, the match was all but over. Now, Jack knew how those poor bastards felt!

Carmen squeezed him to his chest with a loud, "What are you doing? Feeding the fucking birds?"

Bruno, whose only sound was usually a grunt mixed with a quick nod, actually smiled as he said, "Glad you're back in da city, Jack."

As they drove into the midtown tunnel, Carmen announced his proposal.

"Look, when you graduate from college, even though I still don't know why the fuck you want to go, I'll set you up with a job if you want. Our man in Boston, Johnny Sacco, has his stubby fingers in every pie in that city. I won't talk about it again, but always remember you don't have to go to no fucking employment agency or interview for some fucking flunky job.

"One other thing … you'll be wanting to buy a new set of wheels when you get home. Decide what you want, and let me know. Johnny and his associates run the finest midnight auto operation in the country, and you won't be making any fucking monthly payments!"

Bruno pulled up in front of a small grocery store on Ninth Avenue near 42nd Street. Cheese and salami hung from the ceiling like Christmas ornaments, and the sharp aroma of an Italian marketplace jabbed your appetite. Carmen led the way to the back of the store, and beckoned Jack through a curtain.

Five small tables filled the room, and a Peter Lorre lookalike welcomed Carmen with obvious delight. The meal and homemade wine made Jack's favorite Italian dinner of a year ago seem like the blue plate special at George's Café in Newton Corner. After hugs from the owners, they headed for *The Plaza.*

"Let's have a dreammaker before we hit the sack."

Carmen ordered two double Annisettes, and they sank into a couch in the corner of the lounge.

"O.K., Mr. Civilian. You're worried about getting into college. Don't be", grinned Carmen. "So your marks in high school were lousy. That was well over three years ago, and you're no longer a kid with no direction. You're a fucking war hero with the G.I. bill. You'll be accepted at college, no strain. Where do you want to go? You want the Ivy League? That can be taken care of, too."

"C'mon, Carmen. I wouldn't stand a chance!"

"Hey, my cousin Vincent was practically a genius, and Harvard wouldn't give him the time of day. Too many vowels in his name for that Cambridge blueblood joint. With a little investigating, our associates in Boston found that the assistant Dean of Admissions was slippin' the salami to some foreign exchange broad from Sweden. It was pointed out to him that his wife and family and Board of Directors at the institution wouldn't appreciate his fucking Miss Sweden!

"Vinnie became an Ivy Leaguer real fast, and the funny thing was that within a few months he was banging the Swedish bombshell. Her idea of 'exchange student' was a little different from what the fucking educators had in mind.

"Then, there was the time Al Guzzola's son applied for Columbia Law School right in New York. Turned down flat! However, one of the most highly respected law professors there happened to be a lover of the ponies. He spent practically every Saturday at Aqueduct betting every race, and always had action during the week through some high-class bookie. We, of course, owned the bookie, so knew every move he made.

257

"The professor dropped his automobile off at valet parking one sunny Saturday, and headed for the V.I.P. lounge at the big 'A'. Some new concrete sidewalks were being poured in the parking area, and a cement truck accidentally filled the professor's new Buick with concrete. The legal eagle horseplayer was told that if young Mr. Guzzola wasn't one of the chosen few at Columbia, his next automobile would be filled with concrete with him in it, and laid to rest in the Hudson River!

"He didn't need a fuckin' jury to decide that verdict. Al is now a full time lawyer with our family in New York. See what I mean, Jack? Just decide where you wanna go, and if you need a helping hand, you got it. That's all I'm saying."

The Boston flight out of LaGuardia was at noon. Over breakfast, Carmen and Jack talked about the days at Parris Island. Bruno picked them up at ten sharp to make it to the airport in plenty of time. Seeing the Northeast Airline terminal was a welcome sight for Jack. It meant that he was almost home, and Carmen could see that he was anxious to board the plane.

"Well, Goombah," smiled Carmen. "You've come a long way from Yemassee to Vegas and back. You've kept your weapon clean, always carried a pair of clean socks, and you've field stripped those fucking cigarettes. College will be a piece of cake for you, and if you want Ivy League instead of Boston U., just let

258

me know. I still say you're wasting your time, and if you find I'm right, just give Uncle Carmen a call!"

The hug sent Jack onto the plane with the warm feeling of a great friendship.

Chapter 58

It was good to be home, but life had changed drastically for Jack. Sleep never came easily, and his nervous system seemed to always be working overtime. He didn't seem to have anything in common with anyone, and was more of a loner than usual. Well, Al Garbetti would be home in a month or so, and then things would change.

The more he drank, the more the nightmares brought him back to the trenchlines, incoming, and the meat market. Korea was thousands of miles away, yet he was still there each and every day hoping to eventually leave those barren hills and put that time behind him.

"Jack, it's for you", smiled his mother.

It must be Carol calling about her flight from California for Christmas, thought Jack, as he picked up the phone.

"I can't hear you, Shitbird!"

Jack lit up like the Christmas tree in the living room.

"Carmen! Jesus, I'm glad you called! Where are you?"

"I'm at the Sicilian, but I'm heading up your way in a couple of days. Bruno is driving me to Providence for a visit with our friends up on the hill, then to Sabbitini's in the North End in Boston for another visit. I've got a suite at *The Ritz,* and you got one, too. Thought you and Carol would like a couple of holiday nights away from the family, if you know what I mean. Besides, I miss you and your Boston accent, and I've got an opportunity for you for the new year. Like the want ads always say, 'It's the opportunity of a lifetime'!"

"Can't wait to see you and Bruno, Carmen, and to hear what a guy from Brooklyn has in mind for the man from Beantown!"

The Admissions Department at Boston University went out of their way to accept recent Korean War veterans into their Business School program, and Jack thanked them for their positive decision. He'd work for the next nine months, then enter B.U. in September of 1954.

The walk across Commonwealth Avenue from the Admissions Office to the downstairs establishment, 'The Dugout', took all of about two minutes. The place smelled like the basement of your house on a hot day in July. The draft beer was just as musty as the air, but after a couple, a few more seemed to be in order. The thought process always seems to operate better in the atmosphere of a watering hole for some reason.

The Jackie Gleason lookalike bartender pushed another draft, on the house, Jack's way.

"You at the smart factory across the street?"

"Well, I will be, I guess. I've got the G.I. Bill. Might as well take advantage of it, I suppose."

At that very moment, even before the words had cleared his voice box, Jack had major doubts about what route he would really travel the next week, let alone the following September. The only sure bet at the moment was that he was seeing Carmen tomorrow at *The Ritz.*

Marines always seem to work things out together, so we'll take it from there. Maybe Al Garbetti would enjoy meeting Carmen in a few weeks. Who knows what a get together like that could bring about? thought Jack.

About the Author

Jack Orth was born in Boston, MA in 1931. In 1950, he volunteered for the U.S. Marine Corps, and served with the 1st and 2nd Marine Divisions. During the Korean War, he received three

Purple Hearts for wounds received in action, and a Bronze Star medal with Combat V.

In 1954, he attended Boston University. He enjoyed a long career in business to business publishing in advertising sales. For many years he wrote a column for New England Advertising Week, a monthly business newsletter, and guest columns in Marine Corps publications.

He and his wife, Sally, have four children and three grandchildren, and are now retired in Jacksonville, Florida.